Love Stories

His. Hers. Theirs.

You're Dating Him?

A. GERSH

BANTAM BOOKS
NEW YORK · TORONTO · LONDON · SYDNEY · AUCKLAND

RL: 6, AGES 012 AND UP

YOU'RE DATING *HIM?*
A Bantam Book / August 2001

Cover photography by Barry Marcus

Produced by 17th Street Productions,
an Alloy Online, Inc. company.
151 West 26th Street
New York, NY 10001.

ISBN: 0-553-49373-6

Visit us on the Web! www.randomhouse.com/teens

Published simultaneously in the United States and Canada

Bantam Books is an imprint of Random House Children's Books, a
division of Random House, Inc. BANTAM BOOKS and the rooster
colophon are registered trademarks of Random House, Inc. Bantam Books,
1540 Broadway, New York, New York 10036.

PRINTED IN THE UNITED STATES OF AMERICA

OPM   0 9 8 7 6 5 4 3 2 1

To Victoria Carol Velazquez

Prologue

I CAN REMEMBER every single detail from yester-day's horrible morning—who could ever forget it? And ever since that moment—since my parents decided to drop their bombshell and almost cause me to regurgitate bits of my Eggo—I've been obsessing over it. One minute my life is normal, and the next, it's straight out of *The Twilight Zone*. Or a bad soap, I can't decide which.

I'm having a slow morning, per usual. I'm late. My parents are telling me to hurry up, to come and eat because breakfast is "the most important meal of the day." But I'm still getting dressed. *You* try finding an outfit that is both warm and "cool" at the same time! Not exactly an easy task when you live in Edenvale, Minnesota, average winter temp: freeze-your-butt-below-zero Fahrenheit! So here I am, trying to avoid looking like Neil Armstrong when he walked on the moon (as in, total coverage in fattening puff suit) but still hoping to stay warm . . . and I'm thinking this is going to be the hardest part of my day.

Wrong. Not even ten minutes later I am sitting here at the kitchen table, realizing that it doesn't matter what I wear anymore. Nothing matters anymore. Because my life is officially never going to be normal again. At age fifteen I am about to become a sister to someone. *My parents are having a baby!*

Some Christmas present!

I couldn't believe it, and for a while I just sat there, dumbfounded, unable to process the information. But it's true. My mom is eight weeks along. And instead of weeping over what was obviously an accident, she looked happy! Both of them looked happy! And I think both of them expected me to be happy, but instead I just felt like gagging. I remember pushing my plate away, my mouth dropping open like a trapdoor. Most important meal of the day. God, how I hate breakfast!

The rest of the day is a blur. When I wasn't trying to figure out what my crazy parents were thinking, I would come back to one thought—the only thing I know for sure and maybe the only thing I can count on: *Nothing is ever going to be the same again.*

One

Joely

Two months later

"MY PARENTS ARE now baby obsessed twenty-four/seven," I grumbled to my friends as we stood in the cafeteria lunch line at school. "And as if that's not bad enough, my mom is so hormonal, it's scary. One moment she's all sweet, the next she's the Wicked Witch of the West."

I sighed, tucking a strand of my long, dark brown hair behind my ear. My friends, Shelby Masters, Melanie Klein, and Catherine Kwon, tried to make the appropriate sympathetic murmurs, but I could see they just didn't get it. And who could blame them? It wasn't like they'd ever experienced this before. It wasn't like any normal fifteen-year-old had experienced this before.

Because it *wasn't* normal.

I still couldn't get my head around the concept.

3

Even though my mom was quite pregnant now (four months, to be precise), I half expected (and fully hoped) to wake up one morning and find that it had all been a dream. A very funny—in a black-comedy way—dream. But so far, that hadn't happened. So far, the reality of becoming a sister was looming closer and closer. And with each day I became even more miserable.

"A new baby brother or sister . . . ," Catherine mused, her rounded cheeks dimpling into a small smile. "I don't know, Joely. . . . I hate to say it, but it is kinda . . . exciting."

"Exciting?" I spat as we shifted forward in line.

Exciting. That was the word my parents kept using while they babbled away about Baby, all day, every day, starry-eyed as a couple of newlyweds. No doubt they also thought it would be exciting for me to be the baby's built-in baby-sitter. Spending all those *exciting* days at home, changing diapers.

Diapers! I shook my head, trying to clear the image (I was, after all, about to have lunch!), but it stuck there. Gloomily I picked up my lunch tray and wondered, for the thousandth time, what my parents were thinking. It wasn't just that they're too old to have a baby (although they kept insisting that if Mother Nature gave them one, then they were young enough to have one!) . . . but they're also too busy. My dad is a workaholic neurologist, and my mom is an art teacher at the community college.

I barely get any time with them, I thought miserably as night after night of making my own dinner

4

scrolled by . . . *and now I have to share them?*

"Joels," Shelby said matter-of-factly as we studied the lunch "special"—blobs masquerading as macaroni and cheese. "I've told you before, and I'll tell you again: I think you're being way too neg on this. And way too hard on your parents."

I rolled my eyes. Shelby is my best friend, but Shelby lives in Shelbyland and has always had a hard time putting herself in anyone else's shoes. "Too hard on my parents," I muttered, but gave up after that. How could I explain without sounding needy, or jealous, or like a loser? How could I explain that in fact, this new development in the Carmichael family was hardest on *me?*

Perhaps to everyone else the baby sounded exciting, and cute, and fun. . . . But *they* wouldn't have to endure nights of screaming, days of babysitting and housekeeping. . . . I felt exhausted just thinking of it. My mom isn't the most domestic mom in the world, and now she's going to manage a new baby? *I don't think so!* My mom had been very confident about this part, telling me that we'll have "so much fun" with the new baby, but I could smell disaster, and boy, did this ever reek!

"I can see this being a huge shock," Melanie chimed in, looking superserious behind her mop of strawberry blond curls. "I mean, you've been in shock for, like, two months now."

Thank you! One for Joely's team! At last someone was being supportive. And now the others were getting it too, adding in a few coos of sympathy, at least attempting to see the pitfalls, attempting, maybe, to understand that I was about to take on a huge responsibility at the tender age of fifteen.

"But still, J., I think when it actually happens, you'll find it's not the end of the world," Melanie finished.

Grrr! I frowned at my so-called ally, then eyed the two unappetizing choices at the cold "buffet"— make that *barf*et. Cold chicken-noodle salad or tuna with celery. I was thinking about what Melanie had said and tried to figure out which would end up being worse: enduring the pregnancy or what would come next. The pregnancy part was bad; that much I knew for sure. There was living with Mom's mood swings and baby obsession, not to mention the small fact that it was . . . well . . . *embarrassing.* My mom parading her growing bump proudly, my dad strutting around at parties and in front of my friends' parents, talking about "happy accidents!"

"You know, Joely, Michael Douglas recently had a baby, and your dad isn't even close to his age," Shelby ventured as I spooned a gob of tuna onto my plate.

I threw up my hands. *Hello?* Did I really need to explain that my mom wasn't exactly Catherine Zeta-Jones and we couldn't afford the fifty nannies the Jones-Douglas family were no doubt interviewing at that very moment?

"I guess I can't expect you guys to understand," I said finally as I grabbed a bowl of lime green Jell-O. "But let me tell you, a new baby in the family is no picnic."

"I know what you mean," a voice broke in behind me. Deep, male voice. Deep, sexy male voice.

I turned around, surprised—make that *amazed*—to see who was talking to me. Only Ricky Lenci. The cutest junior in school.

"I heard your conversation," he said, pulling me by the arm out of the line and staring intensely at me. "And I get it. Why you're upset, I mean," he added while I tried to swallow and look casual, which is difficult around Ricky. *His eyes are exactly the color of my lime Jell-O . . . ,* I couldn't help thinking. "My sister's knocked up," Ricky whispered bleakly. "It's wrecking my life too."

"Wow . . . crazy," I said, trying not to sound like a dork but ending up sounding totally uncool. It's not easy to talk to the coolest, most untouchable guy in the class. The guy who always wears black leather and who never seems to care if he fails. The guy who rides a Harley and dates women at least three years older than he is. It's especially not easy when you're me. The girl who always studies for every test. The girl whose only experience with motorcycles was on the miniature twenty-five-cent-a-ride cycle outside the KwickPick Mart when I was a tot.

"I don't know why I'm telling you this," Ricky murmured, brushing a hand through his dark hair while my friends gaped at us in the background. "I guess because no one else understands."

"Know what you mean," I confirmed grimly. How well I could relate to that!

7

"My folks are freaked," Ricky continued moodily as I pictured his glamorous older sister, Carla, who was a senior at our school. *She* was pregnant? What, was it something in the air here in Edenvale? "So I just wanted to say . . . I feel bad for you," Ricky finished.

"Thanks," I murmured. Ricky Lenci felt bad for me.

And for the first time all morning, I felt . . . pretty good.

Ricky

"The square of the hypotenuse is equal to . . . ?"

Mr. Bailey searched the room for the answer, and I slouched farther down into my chair. Not that it mattered. Bailey wouldn't call on me for an answer. He hadn't called on me in an entire year of math because he was a smart guy and didn't waste his breath. As far as I knew, the square of the hypotenuse was equal to the four squares in the front row of this classroom with their arms raised. Who knew? Who cared?

I take that back. I wished I did know something about the hypotenuse. Maybe if I knew, I'd have something to think about other than this crap with Carla. This unbelievable mess was so heavy to think about that it made me slouch even more than usual.

How could she be so stupid! It was a statement more than a question by this point. I mean, what

8

was the use of asking questions when your sister was six months pregnant? The deed was done. You could shout about birth-control methods all you wanted, but the reality was about to pop out, and no good was going to come from wondering. . . . But still . . . *duh!*

Carla was always the smart one. She has my mom's smoldering Sicilian looks, and so a lot of people think she's just a dumb beauty. But she's not. Carla's always been a good student. Sure, she's never been an angel, but she's one of those people who can party all night and then ace the exam the next day.

Not that any of that mattered anymore. Carla's future was sealed. She wouldn't be claiming any scholarship to the U. of Wisconsin at Madison to study literature. She'd be too busy with the baby.

I picked up my pencil, held it high above the desk, and pictured the Lenci family's one hope at having a college-educated member. . . . *And we present to you . . . Carla Diana Lenci,* I envisioned the principal saying at this year's graduation ceremony, *and . . . oops, sorry, folks, she didn't make it! And she can forget about college.*

Not that I think college is the Big Dream. I mean, I'm not my parents. That stuff doesn't mean a whole heck of a lot to me. But I know it meant something to them and to Carla. Which is why everyone was screaming at each other all day, every day (and night) at our house. Tempers went through the roof when Carla announced the bad news. And they've pretty much stayed there ever since. Sobbing, screaming, that's all I ever hear. . . .

"Is there going to be another test this week?" Kathlyn Masters broke into my thoughts. I considered spitballing her, then decided she was too young to take it. But jeez, did that kid ever bug the living hell out of me. She's, like, twelve and taking a junior math class. Her sister, Shelby, takes AP college-level math or something. All in the family.

But if the Misses Masters are a cliché of Nerdsville, then we Lencis were becoming a cliché of working-class Italian Americans. My parents had busted their backs for years in the restaurant, and now my sexy Sophia Loren–looking sis was knocked up.

My parents had always hoped that Carla would show the town that the Lencis could make more than meatballs. But they didn't mean she should make babies instead. And as if getting pregnant wasn't bad enough, the guy who got her that way— her boyfriend, Pete—ran the other direction. That was to be expected, I guess. Fancy parents, acceptance into Yale . . . it's an old story. Pity that I'm the one who has to live with it, though. Carla crying all freaking day, my parents wondering how to feed five mouths . . .

"Want to ride after?"

Jake Ramirez kicked me, and I looked up at my buddy. Jake was just like me. All about motorcycles. Feeling the wind on your face. Feeling like you're going somewhere . . .

"Yeah. Count me in," I told him.

I was ready to get going right then. Ride around, then hit some bars, shoot some pool, maybe. Anything to avoid going home to that screaming, fighting mess.

In fact, that's all I wanted to do—avoid home. It was much easier to just split from that scene. It's not as if anyone noticed when I was there anymore. And since my dad had been holding down the restaurant just fine on his own these past few weeks, it was like I wasn't needed at all. Which was cool. Or at least, that's what everyone said. And I guessed they were right. It was great to have your parents obsess over the other loser kid instead of you. For a change. Now my old man didn't even ask to see my report card. I figured they had more on their minds than my terrible academic record. . . . *Hmmm, on second thought, maybe this baby stuff isn't all bad!* I told myself.

"Oh, wait." I frowned at Jake, suddenly remembering that I'd told Joely Carmichael I'd grab a Coke with her. "It'll have to be later," I said. "Got to hang somewhere."

Jake raised an eyebrow, but I ignored him. Too hard to explain. And why should I? It wasn't like a big deal or anything. Call it Baby Blues Anonymous. Or whatever. But Joely and I could relate, even if we had nothing else in common. Even if my friends thought it was funny that I had anything to say to such a straight arrow. And her friends . . . well, who knew what they thought?

11

They were probably terrified I'd get Joely into some kind of trouble if she spent any time with me. We're talking about a very sheltered crowd here. The kind of girls whose idea of "dangerous" was getting a temporary tattoo.

I shifted away from Jake's curious eyes. This would be the second time Joely and I talked this baby thing through. I'd felt better after the first time. It helps to vent, especially with someone who has nothing to do with your world. That way you don't feel like you're exposing your feelings to someone who could come right back and use it against you sometime in the future.

"And I will expect everyone to be ready for the quiz . . ."

I forced Bailey's voice from my head and thought about how much my life sucked. Would it always suck this much?

You know what's weird? Take a girl like Joely. A girl who has everything. Rich parents, good looks, perfect grades. Then the baby thing.

I guess stuff happens to everyone.

Joely

"I like the Baby Björn," Mom commented as she unclasped the blue sling and looked at me and my dad. "Side sling or back sling? It's gotten much more complicated since Joely was born," she added with a smile. "What do you two think?"

I blinked at my mother. *What do I think? I want to get out of here is what I think! I want different parents is what I think!*

That last thought made me feel kind of guilty, so I shot my mom a weak smile to compensate. But I couldn't help these thoughts, and right now I was tired. Tired of walking around and around the mall shopping for—who else?—the baby!

Mom and Dad chattered away to the salesperson, and then, finally, we managed to leave the store, my arms weighed down with bags because my dad couldn't manage carrying the entire inventory of Babyland and my mom was, well—my mom was carrying her own load.

"Oh . . . look!" Mom lit up with a dreamy smile as a young mother came into view, sitting on a bench, a newborn peeking out of her coat. "Oh . . ." Mom brought a hand to her face as the baby began to gurgle, and the young mother looked up and smiled. "What an angel!"

I was about to roll my eyes when in horror I noticed that the woman was actually *nursing* the baby. In public! And worse, my mother was now engaged in a mother-to-mother chat. It was incredibly, incredibly gross.

Instead of rolling my eyes, I squeezed them shut.

"I hope Mom isn't going to do that," I muttered to my father.

"Do what?" my dad queried absently. That's Dad—at the best of times he's not wildly clued in to reality. Most of the time he's thinking about his

13

patients, which makes him the most caring neurologist in the world . . . but not the most switched-on dad.

"That." I opened my eyes and gestured toward the nursing mother, trying to be subtle (not one of my strong suits). "Breast feeding in public. It's—"

"—natural," my mother finished my sentence cheerily as she rejoined us. "Perfectly natural, Joely. Of course when I was pregnant with you, everyone was very prudish about these things, but thankfully we're more advanced nowadays. . . ."

Oh God! I groaned inwardly as we began to patrol the mall in search of an Audio City so that my parents could buy baby monitors. Except that my mom couldn't go five steps without spotting a baby, or a toddler, or a pregnant mother. They were everywhere! Like some kind of secret club, the mothers could spot each other through the crowds and then they'd home in for chats, leaving me vowing I would never have a baby.

"Never?" My dad prodded gently. "Joely, don't you know you should never say never?" he joked. But I couldn't even crack the ghost of a smile.

"But look at them," I retorted as my mother stood talking to a very pregnant woman with long blond hair, whom I remembered was once my mom's yoga teacher, before all this baby stuff began. "They're totally obsessed. They're *baby*washed."

"Just excited," my mother replied as she came over. "Not obsessed, excited." What was it about Mom? She could always tell when I was talking about her and she always had a better answer than I did, making me seem like a spoilsport. "You'll see one day, Joely. It's a wonderful thing, being pregnant. Bringing new life into the world . . ."

"Hmmph!" I made a face behind my mom's back and then struggled to get a grip on my packages. Not that Mom and Dad were kind enough to wait up. In fact, they didn't even notice, just forged ahead, leaving me—their personal porter—to bring up the rear while they drifted through the mall, chatting away in a befuddled baby bliss, gazing lovingly at each other like teenagers. At one point they even almost semismooched. God, I *so* hoped no one I knew was nearby.

"Carmichael!"

I froze. Then slowly, heart knocking like a gong, I turned and saw the source. Just as I'd thought. And feared. Ricky Lenci.

Why does the earth never open up and swallow you? Why is it that some crazy things can and do happen (middle-aged people having babies), but then others (earth swallowing humans) don't? I was wondering this while I forced a smile to my face and tried not to look too much like a total nerd in front of Ricky. But how could I disguise it? There I was, loaded down with diapers and pacifiers and whatever else was in those pale pink Babyland bags, and behind me were my canoodling, *pregnant* parents, who had also come to see who was calling out the family name.

Cringe. Die.

15

"Hey, Carmichael!" Ricky called out in his gruff, sandpapery voice. He was standing near the fountain with some of his friends. Cool, scary, older-crowd people. Instantly I lit up like a halogen lamp—practically neon, I was so embarrassed to be seen in the mall with the parents. On a *Saturday,* no less! But my blushing also came, I have to admit, out of flattery. I was kind of flattered that Ricky had developed a nickname for me. Carmichael. Okay, so it's kind of boyish to be called by your last name, but I liked it. We were buddies. Bros. Or something like that.

"Hey!" I waved at Ricky and noticed my parents exchange "that look." Every kid knows that look: the big warning signal in that international parent language of coded gestures and expressions. The look that says: Here comes trouble, and our daughter is walking straight toward it.

Usually I try to avoid trouble. I've been avoiding trouble pretty much my whole life, so I probably don't get "that look" as much as some people do. I don't like to think of myself as a boring, goody-two-shoes type, but somehow I've always been the kind of kid who listened to their parents when it came to the big stuff. I don't drink. I don't smoke. I "just say no" and all of that. My grades are always good. I make my bed without being asked.

I don't know, maybe it's because I grew up in a very focused, career-oriented house, so I've pretty much been on the straight and narrow all the way. Did I mention I never date the "wrong" guys?

16

Did I mention I never date? (Okay, I've had a few dates, but I'm not exactly the most experienced junior out there.)

So normally, I wouldn't be a point of interest for someone as edgy as Ricky Lenci. But right then I was Carmichael. Ricky's buddy. And for a moment that seemed like the only thing that mattered. Yeah, my parents were all pale and fidgety, and I could see Ricky's posse looking me up and down, half amused and half critical that he'd even know someone like me. But I didn't care. I could only be excited, especially since Ricky had actually left the fountain and was walking over!

"Mom, Dad, this is Ricky Lenci," I said.

"Pleased to meet you." My mom was a little frosty on her greeting, and I could see her miss-nothing gray eyes taking in Ricky's appearance. Especially the tattoo on his forearm (eagle).

"Ricky, hi." My dad was friendlier, but I could see by the alert look in his eye that he was not pleased. My dad may be the kindly scientist type, but he's old school and didn't want his daughter mixing with kids who come from the "wrong side of the tracks."

I've always hated those kinds of expressions. But I'd never had much cause to get my parents to talk about their prejudices. I mean, it's not as if someone like Ricky had ever paid attention to me before. But there's a first time for everything, as they say.

"You want to hang out with us?" That was Ricky. Enough small talk and straight to the point.

"We're just kicking it. At the fountain. You know." He stuffed his hands in his pockets, obviously a little awkward now, and who could blame him? My mom was practically drilling holes into him with her eyes.

I swallowed, looking over at the fountain, where Ricky's people were standing around, wondering if I would feel worse over there than here with my parents.

And suddenly the distance to the fountain felt more than just physical, much more than just a short walk. That distance represented the whole situation with Ricky and me. How we were from different worlds, operated in totally different orbits. Ricky was cool and dangerous and hung out with people in leather. I, on the other hand, apparently hung out with my parents. Not exactly a wild child.

But although I knew Ricky would never go for me—at least not in *that* way—we did have something in common now. The fact was, both our lives were being ruined by other people's babies. And the reality was, Ricky had just asked me—yes, me—to go and hang with him and "kick it," whatever that meant.

"Joely?"

"Huh?" I gaped and gulped like a goldfish. Apparently I was so lost in thought, I hadn't even realized several seconds had passed since Ricky's invitation.

I looked at my parents. They shot me another look. Their "extremely disapproving" look. But I could shoot looks too. And I did. I shot them my "watch me!" look, then I took a deep breath and told Ricky I'd love to hang out with him while my parents finished their shopping.

"See you later," I tossed over my shoulder to my parents, who were evidently shocked that I had so blatantly gone against the grain. I, Joely, the girl who always did right. The perfect daughter and model teen. Now walking off with a leather-wearing, tattoo-bearing tough guy.

But hey, my parents broke the rules by having a baby this late in life. So the way I see it, I can break a few rules too!

Two

Joely

"HELLO?"

I CLOSED the door behind me and sniffed the air suspiciously. Not only was it unusual to have lights on in the house at 6 P.M. on a Monday night (my parents *never* got home this early!), but it was even more unusual to have the aroma of—was it rosemary chicken?—wafting through the house. Definitely a little strange . . . although it sure did smell good.

"Hi, honey!" my mom chirped as I walked into the kitchen.

"Wow!" Was I in another time zone? Mom had an apron on, like moms in fifties sitcoms, and the table was set with our nice china, not the cracked hotelware my dad was obsessed with buying at neighborhood garage sales. Best of all was the rosemary chicken. My favorite! I could smell it roasting in the

21

pan, and there was a dish of scalloped potatoes on the warming plate . . . and sweet peas with butter. Yum.

"Who's coming for dinner? The president?" I asked as I slouched off my giant backpack and proceeded to de-layer.

"No one's coming. Just you, Dad, and me," Mom answered, smiling cheerfully. She looked great too, which was another unusual slant to the evening—not that my mom isn't pretty, but after a hard day's work she typically sat on the couch, looking like Raggedy Ann, while I warmed up yesterday's warmed-up leftovers. Tonight, however, Mom had on gold earrings, which brought out the highlights in her hair, and she had on a beautiful green, silky dress that made her look elegant. Plus she had that glowy-skin thing happening that pregnant women get.

"Special occasion?" I pressed as I grabbed a Coke from the fridge.

"Joely!" Mom paused and held up a wooden spoon. "You act like I never cook!" she chided.

"But you do never cook," I retorted. It was true.

Mom frowned. "Has it really been that long?" I nodded. "Well, I guess it has . . . ," she continued. "I just thought it would be nice to have a proper family dinner. And now that I'm only teaching half-time, I get to do all these fun things, like cook!" Mom patted her stomach triumphantly as if it were the reason for our delicious dinner.

"Hello, girls!" The door slammed, and I looked up to see my dad. Also home early!

"This is so normal, it's disturbing," I murmured

as my dad kissed me on the cheek and then went over to kiss my mom.

Still, I wasn't complaining, and I grinned as my mom handed me a plate piled high to heaven and smelling every bit as good. "This is amazing, Mom," I murmured gratefully through a mouthful of chicken.

As my parents chattered on about Baby this and Baby that, I could really see what Ricky meant when he talked about Total Baby Banter. That's how he described the scene in his house. The dominant theme was always The Baby. Nothing else mattered, and everything began and ended with that one subject. I'd be lucky if this time next week my parents still remembered my middle name.

Thinking of Ricky, however, deepened my smile, made it more genuine. We'd hung out a few times now (not much to report since we didn't do that much talking; we just sorta walked around, and every now and then he'd say something about Babyville at his house and I'd say the same). The fact was, I enjoyed our "talks." I think he liked them too. They were nothing special, I guess, but we had fun.

Things were honest and comfortable between Ricky and me. Maybe because we didn't hang out much in the "real world" (i.e., outside school or with each other's friends). For some strange reason I think that made stuff easier between us.

So there I was, at the table, thinking of Ricky. . . . I confess, it wasn't just our conversations I was visualizing. It was also his intense, deep green eyes and his very high cheekbones.

"Joely? Earth to Joely?"

"Huh?" I blinked at Mom as her face swam into focus.

"We were just discussing the name Chloe for the baby if it's a girl," Dad said.

Do we have to discuss names already? I wondered, sighing inwardly. I rolled my eyes and tried to go back to my thoughts of Ricky, but Mom suddenly snapped her head around and glared at me.

"Apparently you're not interested in our conversation, Joely," Mom said sternly, a touch of hurt in her voice. "It's *your* baby brother or sister we're talking about," she added. "So why is it you don't seem interested?"

I felt both my parents' gazes on me, and then I felt a hot, prickly sensation rising up through the inside of my stomach. Anger. I put down my fork and stared back. "Maybe I'm not interested in your conversation because it's *boring!*" I retorted. "Have you thought of that?"

"Boring?" My mother looked like I'd just suggested I was about to marry a martian and move to outer space.

And that's when I lost it. I threw down my napkin and shot to my feet. It was time for the truth. They'd asked for it, and now they would get it. "I'm sick and tired of hearing about the baby!" I shouted, my eyes glazing with anger. "It's all we ever talk about. And I also know you don't care what I think—about the baby's name, or the wallpaper, or anything!" I continued, tears welling up in my eyes. "No one ever asked my opinion when the bright idea to have this baby first came up, so why don't you all stop pretending you care what I think now!"

Tears spilled out onto my cheeks as I turned away from my speechless parents and fled up to my room, where I fell onto my bed and sobbed. The nice dinner was now completely ruined. But that wasn't what I was crying about. I was crying because my mom's cooking a nice dinner was in fact all about her desire to sit and talk about the baby. Cooking my favorite dish was just a way to make me feel included in the baby celebrations, but it was an effort I couldn't appreciate. Clearly Mom and Dad would be happier by themselves, where they could chat away to their hearts' content.

What about me? I wanted to shout as hot tears seeped into my pillow. I couldn't remember the last time my mom had cooked for me and Dad. But now we'd just had dinner for a baby who wasn't even born! If this was how things were prebaby, I knew it would only get worse from here. Soon little Chloe or Maude or Gladys or whoever would make her way into my family. And with her around, there'd be no room for me.

Ricky

"Everything will be okay, don't worry," I tried to console Carla as she sobbed on the couch next to me.

"Okay?" she snarled. "Are you *crazy?*" Her eyes

were red rimmed. "I'm about to have a kid, mister. What the hell would you know about that?"

Hello, hormones! "Nothing!" I held up my hands in defeat. "You're right," I added softly as Carla went into a fresh round of weeping. Meanwhile my mom was in the other room, also weeping, because she and Carla had just gotten into another fight about the baby and what Carla should do to support it. Ma thought Carla should stay at home and work at the restaurant. But Carla wanted to leave the baby with her every morning while she commuted to college in Madison, part-time. *Ridiculous. Selfish. Unrealistic.* These were Ma's words. *Mean. Jealous. Ashamed.* Those were Carla's.

Keep your voices down—you're driving me insane! And those were Pop's. My dad has a low pain threshold and is not a man of many words. Three seconds after that uncharacteristically long speech he was out the door and off to the restaurant.

"Carla . . . ," I began soothingly as she gulped and sniffled. It really was hard to see her that way. Carla had always been so upbeat, always laughing, always attacking life like it was one big dance party. But now she was very pregnant, very scared, and very—

"Put a lid on it, would you, Ricky?"

—very *angry*. Like, all the time.

"Fine!" I snapped back, and grabbed my leather jacket from the coat hook in the hallway. *You're not the only one who has to deal with this!* I wanted to shout, but what did Carla care about anyone else's feelings right now? She was all wrapped up in her own. And although I had tried my hardest to be calm and reasonable—because, well, *some*one in the family had to keep it together—I was fast losing my temper.

So I took my jacket, slammed the door, and headed out to the garage. There was only one thing to do at moments like this. Only one way to unwind when I'm coiled tighter than a spring: take a ride.

I gunned the engine of my Harley, and as I felt the bike kick, felt the smooth pull of it, the growing power of the machine beneath me, the bad vibes began to lift. There is nothing in the world like riding. It's where I feel freest. It's where I think best. It's like the wind just blows all the questions out of my head and anything seems possible.

I took the bike around through the side roads and onto Main Street, then five minutes later I was where I needed to be. Out on the interstate, the gravel speeding beneath me like it was a conveyor belt and I was just going along with it, all resistance draining from my body.

Well, maybe not all resistance. Even as I pumped the speed, I still couldn't get to that light, free feeling. Everything still hung over me, and I felt hopeless and desperate and totally without power. The baby stuff had screwed up a lot of things in my family. We were fine before. So why this now?

I started to think of Joely Carmichael as I pushed my speed and bore down on the horizon, as if I could really ever get there. Joely was all right. She was someone I could vent with. We got each other's raw deal. Everyone else thought it was no big deal. But what would they know?

Thinking of Joely made me feel like I wasn't completely alone in this scenario. But after a while my thoughts got kind of dark. If we hadn't had this common problem, Joely would never even give a guy like me the time of day, and it wasn't just that she was so squeaky clean. She also happened to be from up on the hill, where the rich people lived. These are complicated people. They have standards that guys like me could never hope to meet. Take her parents. Meeting them in the mall was the type of experience that usually I can laugh at after. But when things are bad, that kind of stuff pops into your head and you really feel mad.

All my life I've had people like the Carmichaels look down on people like me. I could see it in their eyes then. Before we'd even spoken, they'd already made up their minds that I was no good. And I wasn't surprised. That's to be expected in this town. People here have always been very segregated: rich professionals like the Carmichaels and the working class, like me and mine.

As I cruised the highway, I wished I could just keep on going. Leave this town for good. Go to a place where nobody cared who was from what class of society. *If a town like that even exists,* I thought as the wind whipped my hair into my eyes.

If a town like that existed, it was probably New York. Or LA. Or maybe even as close as Chicago. Like, only five hours away on this bike if I went without stopping. I'd always wanted to move to a big city. Be an actor, maybe. And as soon as I finished school, I planned on splitting. *Hell, I could go right now.* It was definitely tempting to just keep riding . . . as far away from this place as I could get.

I like old-style film acting. Jimmy Dean in *East of Eden.* Marlon Brando in *Streetcar Named Desire.* Forget all those poser dudes, like Brad Pitt or Matt Damon. Brando and Dean, they were the real thing.

I tried to focus on acting as I rode my bike, trying to tune into something I liked. But then I thought, *If I ever do get to be an actor and make it out to Tinseltown, they'd just stereotype me the way the Carmichaels did. Take one look at me and see some no-good Italiano kid ready to get cast in a mobster movie.* "Fuggedaboudit" and all that crap.

I really hate that shticky Italian stuff. It gives all of us a bad name. . . .

So what are you going to do about it? I asked myself as I sped past factories and warehouses and cornfields, heading for nowhere. And the simple answer was: I didn't have an answer. The way I saw it, the world is out to pigeonhole you. People need to make you out to be a certain way so that they can feel good about themselves. Maybe I couldn't change it. Doesn't mean I had to like it.

And I didn't. In fact, I was going way too fast, getting all pissed off thinking about Joely's parents and picturing myself as an extra on *The Sopranos.* Way too much speed.

But I was past caring.

Joely

"Don't forget, I need all the sign-off sheets from your parents before I can go ahead and book you for the Mathlympics," Ms. Delille reminded everyone as the math-club meeting came to a close.

"Mathlympics. Yes!" Shelby punched my arm, her eyes twinkling as she pictured the Edenvale Mathletes scoring victory in this year's summer Midwestern Mathlympics in Chicago.

Okay, so I know it sounds megadorky, but I can't deny it: I like math. I've always liked math, and I've always been good at it. To me math isn't boring and hard. To me it's kind of cool, like cracking some kind of weird code. I find it sort of satisfying.

"We are *so* going to party. In our *own* room," Shelby muttered excitedly to me, and I smiled, picturing the other, nondorky side of Mathlympics. Hotel rooms. Possible parties being held with possible cute guys. Possible raiding of hotel-room minibar. Granted, I'd never done that before, but with everything my parents had been slinging my way lately, I could see myself breaking into a few miniature vodkas and following the new family motto: Shock the World!

"It's going to be awesome," I agreed, reapplying my Burt's Bees red lip gloss as I waited for the always slow Shelby to collect her stuff and futz with her long, glossy blond hair. Chicago: awesome it would be. I took Shelby's arm, making an extra effort. Lately things had been a bit tense between us, and she'd accused me of having less time for her. Which was maybe a little bit true. I guess I just found Shelby and the other girls too focused within their own happy, trivial worlds . . . while mine felt like it was falling apart. I couldn't talk about hair and makeup and math grades and Carson Daly with all this baby business hanging over me.

And the truth of it was, only Ricky really understood what was on my mind these days. So lately I'd elected not to hit the mall or the movies with the girls. I stayed home instead. Practicing for my future role as baby-minder, I guess. Practicing for the time when I'd have no life. Which was precisely four and a half months away.

But all of that aside, Mathlympics *would* be great, and I grinned and cleared my head as I walked with Shelby, picturing a parentless world of fun in Chicago.

"Is it really *that* windy is what I want to know," Shelby chattered, flicking her hair, but my thoughts had already drifted from being excited about the trip back to feeling maudlin.

Kind of like a last fling with the world of the free, my inner voice reminded me, and my expression changed from one of excitement to one of gloom. The baby would be born midsummer. So what would begin as a summer of fun and freedom would most certainly end in a symphony of baby screams, with diaper Velcro swipes providing the percussion.

"Why so sour?" Shelby demanded as we walked out of the classroom and into the hallway. "You look like someone just offered you a turd sandwich."

"In a way, maybe they did," I mumbled back, picturing myself up to my arms in diaper changing. Ugh!

"Stop fixating on this baby stuff," Shelby advised, giving me a shrewd once-over. "It just gets you on such a downer, Joels. Stop worrying! The baby hasn't even gotten here yet!"

Stop worrying? I stopped midstride and shot Shelby a glare. "It's easy for you to say," I replied, somewhat hurt. After all, Shelby was my best friend. Shouldn't she at least try to fake commiserate with me, even if in fact she thought I was overreacting to the worst, most life-changing news I'd had all year? "I just think," I began, fumbling for words. "I just think you . . . oh, never mind!" I finished, giving up. What was the point? Shelby hadn't understood my trauma from the get-go.

"Look, Joels, either talk to me or don't," Shelby ventured. "I'm just trying to help. But I can't say I'm getting you."

"I can see that," I retorted coldly, and with barely a good-bye I stalked down the corridor and out of the building. *God, the baby is ruining everything,* I thought miserably, trying to keep the tears down. I couldn't connect with my parents anymore, and now I couldn't connect with my best friend. It just wasn't fair.

But at least there was still one person I *could* connect with, and I hoped like crazy I would see him as I "casually" walked through the school parking lot and past the area where kids kept their bikes. My mind was still going a mile a minute, trying to figure out whether Shelby and I could find a way to talk, when . . .

Wow! Ricky looked incredible, sitting on his black-and-red bike. I couldn't help noticing the way his perfectly sculpted, long legs looked. He looked so natural on that monstrous thing and so completely—

"Want a ride?"

I was caught off guard as Ricky turned to look right in my eyes. I hadn't even thought he'd seen me. He'd been talking to Jake Ramirez, Deena McQueen, and some of the senior crowd. But there he was, his emerald eyes looking straight at me.

"English is my language of choice," Ricky joked when I didn't immediately answer.

"Oh . . ." I flushed brighter than a beet salad, my head spinning as I tried to look offhand and relaxed when my heart was in fact racing so hard, I thought I might pass out. Riding with Ricky? On a motorcycle? Definitely dangerous. Definitely totally illegal as far as my parents' law went. They'd have my head on a stick if they ever found out.

Joely

"I can't *believe* you, Joely Carmichael!" My mother was practically bursting my eardrum, she was so hopped up.

"I'm *sorry,*" I murmured, but she continued to

rant, so I just switched off as her Subaru station wagon trundled up the hill to our home.

Grrr! I sighed. Everything about that motorcycle ride had been a total rush. From the thrill of having my arms around Ricky's waist to the floaty way it felt riding around on that machine . . . it had been amazing. Until my mom showed up.

She *would* have to pick this afternoon to see if I needed a ride home from school! And now she was chewing me out. When my mom got on a roll, there might be no end to it. This could go on all night.

". . . Just so irresponsible of you . . . that boy is obviously a bad influence. . . . I could have gone into early labor, I was so terrified. . . ."

I tried to let Mom's words just wash right over me as she assaulted my right ear with her fury, but after a while it became harder and harder to just sit there and take it. She was wailing like a banshee. And all over one lousy motorcycle ride.

"Mom, get a grip!" I shouted back. "We were only riding around the school parking lot! I *said* I was *sorry!*"

I bit my lip. It wasn't in my nature to be shouting at my mother, but lately I seemed to be doing quite a lot of it. *That's because she deserves it,* I told myself. It was true, right? I mean, riding around the school parking lot with a helmet on was hardly living on the edge.

"You're still lucky to be alive," my mom commented in a quieter tone, flicking a searching gaze my way, her gray eyes revealing worry and question.

"Joely, you know your father lost a cousin to a motor-cycle accident! What's going on here? Were you deliberately going against us?"

I stared out the windshield and refused to answer.

She banged at the remote control to open our garage door, her eyes flashing. "I don't know who you are right now, Joely," she retorted impatiently. "You tell me. You're so unlike your usual self. You're always in a bad mood, you've stopped hanging out with your usual friends. . . . Are you still upset about the baby? I thought we'd covered that!"

I narrowed my eyes into slits as we drove into the garage and sat in the dark in silence, each of us digesting our own thoughts.

My mom evidently thought that the baby stuff could be wiped away by a few cheerful moments. After our dinner disaster she'd simply smiled brightly at me the next day and fixed me raspberry pancakes. That didn't fix anything.

"Look, Joely," my mom began, running a hand through her hair and sighing. "The pregnancy was an accident, yes, and it's going to be a tough adjustment for all of us . . . but can't you be just a little bit supportive even if you can't be joyful?"

I cranked open my car door, feeling a surge of fresh anger. *Once again the baby dominates everything!* Mom and I couldn't even have a fight on our own without the baby issue taking over. "Why can't you just admit you're obsessed?" I muttered as I stomped through the mudroom and kicked off my boots.

"And why can't you admit you've changed?" Mom shot back, bringing up the rear. "Joely!" She stopped me with a hand on my shoulder.

I wheeled around. "What?"

"Why won't you *talk* to me?" Mom stared at me so deeply, I felt uncomfortable and shifted my gaze. What did she mean anyway? I *was* talking to her, wasn't I?

"We used to be able to communicate. You never used to treat me like the enemy," she added in a hurt voice.

I shrugged. What could a person say to that? Sure, it was partly true. Even though Mom and I didn't get to spend much time together, during what little time we had between school and her job, we used to get on much better. But that was before . . .

"Is it this Ricky boy?" Mom demanded as I unzipped my coat. "Maybe you're spending too much time with him."

Now I really rolled my eyes. As in, did a full eyeball roll from corner of socket to corner of socket. *Trust her to blame all of this on a guy she barely even knows.* Now, that was paranoia! Or hormonal imbalance.

"Honey, it does seem like since you met him, you've shut everyone else out," Mom continued as I stomped out of my winter boots.

"I've only hung out with him once or twice!" I yelled, and stalked up to my room. *Argh!* I was so mad, I hurled myself onto my bed like it was a punching bag and I was all fist. *Spending too much time with him* . . . my mother's words echoed through my skull. It was ridiculous. Ricky and I barely ever hung out, and everyone in my universe seemed to be having a palpitation over it. For starters, there was Shelby. At first she and our other friends Melanie and Catherine were all excited for me that a cute guy like Ricky would look my way. But now Shelby was being all weird over it if I mentioned Ricky's name more than once during a conversation.

And now Mom. God, it was so supremely annoying! *Can't I have a new friend without flipping everyone out?*

I lay on my bed like a lump for a full ten minutes, listening to Mom rustling around downstairs in the kitchen, making tea, which caused me a pang of guilt. She was pregnant, and I should be making her tea. But I let it go. She'd upset me anyway—she should be making *me* tea! And then I heard her murmuring on the phone. No doubt to Dad.

"And Joely . . . mumble mumble . . . Joely . . . that Ricky kid . . . mumble mumble . . . ," I heard her mutter.

I sat up, walked over to the stairwell, and strained my ears to catch what she was saying.

"I think she just needs some extra-special attention," Mom said.

I smiled a little on the stairway and, when Mom hung up, went back inside my room. Extra-special attention. Call me greedy, but I liked the way that sounded. . . .

Three

Ricky

"WHAT DO YOU think, Rick? Repairable? Or one for the scrap heap?" Spike asked me as he cocked his head and looked at the mangled bike that some old guy had just brought in.

"We could give it a shot," I replied, and Spike nodded.

Spike is my boss. Doesn't much sound like a boss's name, but then, Spike isn't much like your regular boss. He's more like a big brother or something.

I've been working on and off at Spike's Bikes since I was a kid. The man has always treated me well and valued my opinion. Like now. It always made me feel good when Spike asked me what I thought. Made me feel appreciated for working hard.

There's only one thing I've ever worked hard at in my life, and it's fixing bikes. I've busted my butt over those things, crouched on my knees with a wrench in one hand and a soda in the other, spending my afternoons in a haze of grease and oil.

But I love it, so I do it. There's something rewarding about fixing something that's broken. You get these old pieces of junk in there, and you could swear their lives are long over. But then you tinker around and try a few things and bingo! Like new.

Mostly I liked the silence of working with bikes. Me and Spike, we never talked all that much. Now and again Spike asked me about girls or life or whatever, but for the most part it was all about the bikes.

"How's school, Rick?" (One of those now and agains, I guess.)

I looked up from wheeling the mangled bike into the garage and grunted. School. Not my favorite subject. In fact, the more I thought about it lately, the more I figured I might not even stay through my junior year. Why wait to flunk when you could just walk?

"I'm gonna quit, I think," I finally said to Spike when he kept pressing me on the subject. "Get my GED later."

"Quit?" Spike wrinkled up his already sunwrinkled forehead until he looked like a California raisin. "Sounds like a pretty dumb idea," he added, wiping grease-stained hands on his overalls.

"Dumb?" I grinned. "You didn't finish high

school, and you've made your dreams happen. So you've got no leg to stand on there."

"Okay, okay," Spike shot back in his raspy, too-many-cigarettes voice. "But kid, I did a lot of things I regret," he added. "Not finishing school was one of them."

"Huh." I tried to focus on taking apart the bike. It was kind of unusual for Spike to open up to me about his own life, and it sort of made me uncomfortable. But also flattered that he was telling me personal stuff like that. I could see he wasn't too good at talking about this stuff (like me), but somehow it mattered to him to tell me what he thought. And that was pretty cool. Especially since no one in my family much seemed to care what I did these days.

"You've only got one year left," Spike continued, wiping down his tools. "So what's the big deal?"

I shrugged. "That place and me . . ." I struggled to explain my feelings about school. "It's like oil and water," I added as my eye fell upon a can of grease. "I hate being there, and nothing interests me. The only thing I like is . . . drama class," I admitted finally, wondering if Spike would think I was some kind of wuss for liking drama. But I did like it. I'd been in last year's school play, but this year it was some kind of stupid musical, so I stayed clear.

"Plays?" Spike's sun-creased face broadened into a smile. "Good for you, kid. A regular Jimmy Dean, you could turn out to be."

41

"Yeah?" I tried not to look too pleased.

"I think you should stay in school, Rick," he repeated. "Otherwise I'm dead sure you'll regret it later on in life. When you're my age, for instance."

"I don't see what's so bad about quitting," I argued as Spike lit up a Marlboro. "That way I can get on with life faster instead of wasting away in this dump of a town."

"Let me tell you something." Spike looked at me with his piercing blue eyes, and I shut my mouth. Spike wasn't a big talker, but that meant when he did speak, he'd thought it through real well. Unlike most people.

"Quitting doesn't get anyone anywhere. If you want to have an interesting ride in this life, Rick, you have to make it over the speed bumps before you can get out onto the open road. Nothing good comes easy, but if you stick it out, the good stuff comes to you in the end."

I wiped a blob of grease off my cheek and considered what Spike had said. It made some sense. I could see what he was driving at, at least.

"Think about it?" Spike asked.

"Yeah." I nodded curtly, and then we went back to fixing the bike like we'd never started this heavy conversation. But while we worked, Spike's words cut through my thoughts. *Nothing good comes easy.* . . . Maybe walking out on school wasn't such a great idea. Especially since I had only one year left.

I thought about my life, and then I thought about my friends, like Jake and Andy Swensen and Deena

42

and the rest of them. They were cool and all, but they had no dreams, not as far as I could tell. The girls only cared about what they looked like, and the guys only cared about booze and sex and bikes. Only Joely seemed to have anything unusual to say for herself. *That girl has energy,* I thought, and then I wondered why I was thinking of her in the same breath as analyzing my friends. Joely wasn't exactly a friend.

But the more I thought about it, the more I realized I couldn't really define *what* Joely was to me. I knew what she wasn't: definitely not girlfriend material. But she wasn't a friend either. I mean, it wasn't like we hung out together on a regular basis or anything. So what was she?

Just some random rich girl, then, I figured. That had to be it. Joely was just some random girl I knew and occasionally shot the breeze with . . . right?

As far as definitions went, that was about the best I could do. But "random girl" didn't quite fit. *Like me and Joely,* I thought with a half smile, and got back to work.

Joely
Names My Parents Are Considering for the Baby

<u>Girl</u>	<u>Boy</u>
Chloe	Lyle
Zoe	Earl
Carmen	Jeffrey
Jemimah	Kirk
Caitlin	William
Michelle	James
Eloise	Joshua

Joely

"I mean, what is the *point* of a baby monitor?" I babbled to Ricky at Friday lunch, picking at my tuna-salad sandwich. "It seems like extra punishment," I continued. "As if hearing the baby crying all the time isn't bad enough. Now they want a walkie-talkie to alert them to more cries?"

"Yeah," Ricky agreed. "You'd think they'd want to tune out the brat whenever possible. Ignorance is bliss, right?"

"No kidding! But *not* according to my parents." I shook my head with disgust. "They've already bought, like, fifty of them and installed them throughout the house." I was exaggerating, of course, but I was making Ricky laugh. Which made me feel good. Joking around was my way of relieving the self-consciousness I felt sitting with Ricky in the cafeteria.

Don't get me wrong. When he'd motioned me over to sit with him at an empty table, I was psyched. But still, I couldn't help feeling a little bit self-conscious. Ricky's just so cool and laid-back, and I'm . . . well . . . I'm not naturally cool like Ricky. And it didn't help to have Shelby, Catherine, and Melanie eyeballing us from their table on the one side of the cafeteria. And Ricky's friends eyeballing us from the other!

"So, is Carla scared about the delivery?" I asked Ricky, anxious to get back to talking after I caught him looking moodily toward his friends. For a moment I thought he might say "see ya" to me and go off and join them, but then he flashed me a huge grin and began telling me this hilarious story about Carla and how the Lamaze instructor had told her she was the most "difficult" mother-to-be she'd ever encountered. I almost cried with laughter. Ricky has a great storytelling ability, and for a moment I forgot my friends and his friends and just cracked up.

". . . but yeah, I guess she is scared," Ricky finished. "We all are," he added, more seriously, and for a moment we were both silent. Carla's baby was due any day now. Ricky held my gaze for a moment, then looked away. Although he had confessed a lot of worry over the baby stuff to me, he also had this way of making light of it, of trying not to let the whole thing get to him. But I could see in his eyes he was even more scared than he'd admitted.

"So . . . Carmichael," he began after a pause during which we both played with our food. "Have your parents forgotten your name yet?"

I laughed. It wasn't *that* bad yet. In fact, they'd been giving me a little "extra attention" for the past few weeks, which was a definite turnaround. "When they're not obsessing over *The House at Pooh Corner,* they're actually making me dinner and renting movies *I* want to watch!" I said. "They're worried I've got this sibling-envy thing," I added.

Secretly I knew their worry had a lot more to do with something else: they feared I was spending too much time hanging out with "the wrong element" (in other words, Ricky) and wanted to keep an eye on me. But of course I didn't want to admit that to Ricky!

"Extra attention. Nice . . . ," Ricky said with a smile. And I found myself admiring his amazingly even, Tic Tac-white teeth. Ricky has an incredible smile in addition to his magnetic eyes, and as he smiled at me, I felt panicked, wondering whether I was going to start blushing! I mean, it's not like I have a crush on him or anything. After all, there'd be no point in having a crush on someone who spends time with you only because you both have the same problem. But . . . sometimes I had to really concentrate on not firing up into a flush in front of Ricky. He has the kind of smile that would do that to any girl. . . .

"Wow, we're freaking them out." Ricky grinned as he spotted Melanie craning her neck to get a good look at us.

I felt my cheeks burn as I spotted Ricky's pal Deena checking me out, looking me up and down with total incomprehension on her face, as in: *What's he doing sitting with that Mathlete nerd?*

I tried to pretend his friends—and mine— weren't gaping at us. But I had a mental Post-it moment: *Tell Shelby and the girls to chill out!* In a way, my friends' stares made me feel enviable (I mean, I *was* sitting with the cutest junior in the school!). But in a different sort of way, I knew the girls thought I was playing with fire—hanging out with one of "them." "Them" being kids who didn't play by the rules.

And I didn't need my friends' overprotectiveness. Ricky and I were just friends. We liked hanging out from time to time and "rapping" (as Ricky called it). And it was a free country, right?

"No, it's *Edenvale High,*" Ricky reminded me when I mentioned liberty and democracy. And I knew exactly what he meant. At Edenvale High, you stuck to your own crowd and who you were was pretty clearly defined.

"Do you think everyplace is this cliquey?" I asked Ricky as I took a small bite of my sandwich.

"No way, uh-uh." Ricky shook his head firmly. Obviously he agreed with me: this place was really conservative! And then Ricky got this kind of long-ing look in his eyes as he mentioned how much he was looking forward to moving to a big city.

"Me too," I retorted, fiddling with my hair (I was still nervous I might blush). *Me too?* Immediately I felt like a liar. I had never really thought about moving to a big city. I'd spent my whole life in Edenvale. . . . *Idiot!* I cursed myself for playacting as Ricky started in about Chicago and LA and New York . . . and I pre-tended to know all three cities well when in fact I barely knew Chicago, had only been to New York once, when I was five, and as for LA? The closest I'd come to California was watching *Beverly Hills 90210*.

I dug my nails hard into my palm until it hurt, try-ing to punish myself for being so fake. But the truth is, this wasn't the first time I'd been a little less than hon-est about who I was in front of Ricky. We'd only hung out a couple of times, but every time I was with him, I noticed I tried harder to be "cool" around Ricky. I'd started throwing in a couple of curse words every now and then. I'd also started wearing a lot more black than usual and heavier eye makeup. Raccoon eyes, accord-ing to Shelby, but I thought I was being more subtle than that. Still. I couldn't deny it. I *was* acting differ-ent. I wasn't always being Joely.

But why not? a little voice inside me stuck up for me as I fiddled with my fork and listened to Ricky wax lyrical about Chicago rock bands I'd never heard of. *What's wrong with a change? What's wrong with loosening up?*

I lifted my chin and tried to act more relaxed,

smiling and nodding as Ricky talked about the bands. And although I knew I was being a poser, I forced away my doubts, tuning out the self-critical parts of me. Where was the crime in change anyway? New makeup, new style . . . I wasn't doing this for Ricky. He was just exposing me to new ways of being myself.

And after being in the same crowd my whole life, it was a refreshing change.

"So who're you listening to, Carmichael?" Ricky broke into my thoughts, his gravelly voice cutting through my inner monologue.

Instantly I froze. Felt myself grow pale as a marshmallow, so that my freckles must have stood out like German measles.

Who was I listening to? Well, right then I was listening to my *heartbeat.* And the darned thing was going faster than a torpedo. "Uh—uh . . . ," I stammered, feeling my mouth grow dry as I scrolled through my list of favorite bands. Dave Matthews. Lauryn Hill. The Corrs. Would he find them too mainstream, would it make him think I wasn't nearly as edgy as him? And of course I would also reveal myself right there as someone who didn't have a clue about any of the bands he'd mentioned but had faked it to seem cool. *Who're you listening to?* God, how I hated that question.

"Frank Sinatra," I blurted, and then immediately squeezed my eyes shut and regretted the fact that I had the power of speech. *Why did you say that?* I berated myself.

Granted, it was true. For some reason I had lately started to listen to my parents' old vinyl stuff and had found myself really getting into Sinatra. But telling Ricky? The secret was out. I had officially in that moment crowned myself: Joely, Queen of the Terminally Unhip!

"Old Blue Eyes!" Ricky growled approvingly. I opened my eyes a smidgen. Was Ricky actually nodding and smiling? "He's the man," Ricky added. *"I've got you under my skin. . . ."*

Oh. My. God. Was it my imagination, or was Ricky Lenci really singing . . . with an amazing old-time crooner voice . . . to me?

I bit my lip, Ricky's husky voice cutting right through me. It was beautiful! And this time I really couldn't help blushing because the lyrics . . . well . . . it was a love song, and that does tend to make a girl blush, even if it's just her buddy singing it.

Ricky did a little bow as he finished. "I love Frank," he added, before taking a slug of his Coke.

"You do an incredible imitation!" I couldn't stop myself from gushing. "You're so talented!"

"Nah." Ricky waved off my praise, ducking his head and looking embarrassed. For my part I was still struck dumb by how good Ricky was at imitating Sinatra. He'd sounded *exactly* like him! And of course I felt saved by my good luck. We apparently both liked Sinatra. A wild, lifesaving coincidence.

"Every Italian American can do Frank imitations," Ricky said. "It's in our blood." Then he smiled ironically and leaned way back in his chair.

50

"There, I've gone and done what I hate most: stereotyped myself."

I tried to look ironic (which is harder than you might think!), but the truth was, I felt a little woozy from Ricky's song. Nobody had ever sung to me. Okay, so maybe he wasn't quite singing *to* me, but—

"Gotta go." Ricky interrupted my train of thought, scrutinizing his bleeping beeper. "Places to be," he added mysteriously, and without another word drifted off.

That's true Ricky style, and I'd gotten used to it. One moment we're chatting, the next he's outta there.

For a second I wondered if it was about Carla since her baby was due.

Nah. He would have told.

Ricky was just being . . . Ricky.

But I didn't feel stiffed. After all, I'd just been serenaded. . . .Well . . . sort of . . . right?

Ricky

"She okay, Pop?" I asked my dad as he burst out of Carla's hospital room, where I could hear all this shrieking and moaning. Ma was still inside, trying to help Carla breathe, and there was no way I was going in. Carla had been in labor for five hours now, and I'd headed straight over as soon as Pop beeped me at lunch. All I'd done was pace, and now I looked to my dad for answers.

"Yeah. Okay." That's Pop—Mr. Conversational. Any info to be gotten here would not come from him, so I peered through the wavy glass of the delivery room, looking for any sign of Carla. Not that I could see her, and I knew that, but I felt better looking in at nothing than doing nothing but listen to her yell.

I swallowed and tried hard not to be nervous. *Carla's a tough cookie—she can handle it,* I told myself. But Carla was also a hysterical person, and she was in labor! Her doctor might get hurt in there!

So I tried to think of something else as I waited for news. My thoughts cut back to Joely. *That kid's a weird one. She's easy to talk to, but . . . why didn't I tell her that Carla was in labor when I got beeped?* Pop had sent a text message, so I knew Carla was in early labor when I looked at my pager. But somehow I kept it to myself. Guess I'm the weird one, not Joely. Although she had been doing some strange stuff to her eye makeup lately. And she's not the kind of girl who even needs makeup.

Girls. Go figure.

Anyway, I realized that I like to keep some things private. Especially when I'm scared. Like now. And I guess I thought I might jinx things by telling Joely about Carla going into labor . . . better to make these announcements when everyone's safe and the drama's over.

But these labor dramas can go on for days. I knew this from Carla's prenatal books. And I went with her to Lamaze once, which was only like the scariest thing in the world. Carla told the instructor she was a moron, and, well . . . the point is, Carla could be in there for days. Maybe even—

"Ricky." I looked up to see Ma standing in the doorway to the delivery room. For a second I didn't recognize her in her cap and gown. But then I saw her big, brown eyes. Full of tears.

"Ma?" I croaked, my heart thudding like a live brick in my chest.

"Dolores?" My dad shot to her side and began shaking her.

"It's a boy! His name is Marco Dylan Lenci."

As Ma said those words, I felt myself go into this hazy head space, relief mixing with panic mixing with all sorts of crazy feelings I didn't even know, so I don't even know what to call them. I was an uncle. There was a baby. Carla was a mother. All these things swirled around in my brain, and I didn't know what to make of them. But they were the truth, and as my mom and dad broke down in tears and rushed into the room to see the baby, I hung back, waiting to get more of a grip.

But suddenly I felt happy and joyful, and I could hear my mom laughing from inside the delivery room. Even though there was a cloud hanging over this baby, this was a big moment. I took a deep breath and walked in.

Marco Dylan. Marco after my granddad. Dylan after Dylan Thomas, Carla's favorite poet. My nephew. The little tyke had made it, and jeez, was he ever the ugliest thing I'd seen. Red face, matted black hair.

But Carla, she looked so different. Calm, for once, and something else too . . . proud?

"Isn't he a beauty?" Ma picked up little Marco, her face lighting up with love.

Carla looked up at me as if daring me to tell the truth: newborns are not beautiful. They are ugly. At least, this little guy was.

But hey, I wasn't going to spoil the mood. My nephew was a fighter. He'd made it through, and as I picked him up, I could see he was a tough guy. "The worst is yet to come, little buddy," I said quietly to the baby. After all, it's only fair that someone should warn Marco what kind of family he's coming into.

But right then, even I had to admit, the family looked good to me. Pop was grinning, Ma was teary eyed, and Carla was holding Ma's hand and smiling at me holding Marco. Not a bad moment, as moments go.

But almost as quickly as the moment came, I felt it drift away. I looked at Marco and thought of all the hard times that lay ahead for us all. We were a bigger family now than we could cope with. Who was going to take care of Marco when there was so much other stuff to consider? How was Carla going to be a mom, for example, when she was still a teenager?

I gave the baby back to Carla and took my feelings outside. Standing in the hallway, I felt so conflicted that I wanted to get out of there. But I couldn't. That wouldn't go over well with Ma. So I took out some change and made a call. Had to tell someone about my new nephew, right?

"No, Joely isn't home," Mrs. Carmichael said in her clipped "uptown" voice.

"Could you tell her to call Ricky, please?" I asked. "It's urgent."

"I'll give her the message," Joely's mom replied, and then hung up just as I was trying to say a polite good-bye.

I walked away from the pay phone and stuffed my hands into the pockets of my jacket. I was disappointed that Joely wasn't home and pictured myself compensating by going for a long motorcycle ride. I needed air. But I am pleased to say I didn't bail. Instead I took a deep breath, looked at the doors to Carla's delivery room, and walked toward it. I didn't really feel up to going in, but there are things you do in life even though you don't want to.

Because you have to.

Joely

My kind of Sunday . . . , I thought happily as I caught the Frisbee my dad flicked toward me.

It had been a perfect morning. The kind of spring day in which you could smell a whiff of summer in the air.

And for the first time in what felt like forever, we'd taken a family picnic out to Bridal Veil Falls, which was a waterfall in this beautiful national park.

Mom had packed all sorts of goodies for lunch, and we'd spent a lazy Sunday enjoying the outdoors. Usually Sundays are all about homework for me, but today was like a break from everything. Even ourselves.

I smiled as I looked at Mom, lying on a rock with a peaceful expression on her face. She and I hadn't fought all weekend. And she looked so happy, just napping in the sun.

She's getting quite whalelike. . . . I couldn't help that thought, and it was true: Mom's belly was sticking straight up as she lay on the rock. All of which reminded me how little time we had left as just us, a family of three.

"That was fun!" Dad patted me on the shoulder as we panted back to the picnic blanket and helped ourselves to cherry cheesecake.

"Finish it before I do," Mom pleaded as she clambered down from the rock and tried to avoid the cheesecake. Cheesecake is her major pregnancy craving, and she's been really worried about gaining weight even though Dad and I both agree: she's all tummy; the rest of her is still as slim as ever.

I happily pigged out on the dessert and then lay on the picnic blanket, my hair fanned out behind me, enjoying the warm rays of sunlight on my face.

"Joely, you always did have such lovely hair," Mom remarked as she came and sat next to me on the blanket.

"Thanks, Mom." I shifted over to make room for her and smiled. She'd been so nice to me all day.

Not once had the conversation turned to my deescalating grades, although my parents had been on my case lately because I got a less than perfect score on the last physics quiz. Naturally they associated this with my "new boyfriend," Ricky, but that's only because they refused to accept the obvious; that is, I couldn't focus on my grades because I was only months away from becoming a full-time baby-sitter! How could anyone get work done with that chaos looming . . . ?

But anyway, today seemed to be truce day. The baby didn't dominate conversation, and as I let my mom braid my hair, I felt grateful that my parents hadn't mentioned my grades again.

"I've always loved your long hair, honey," Mom added as she finished my braid and smoothed it down my back. I waited for a word about my dark eye makeup or a barbed comment about my newly black wardrobe (her other major source of concern). But Mom was on her best behavior, and when she looked at me, there was only an affectionate smile. And as we packed up for the day and headed toward the car, I felt pleasantly light-headed and without worry. For once everything was okay with us as a family. And it felt good for a change.

"So . . . how are your friends . . . besides, uh, this new boy, I mean?" Dad asked nervously, and then cleared his throat as he started the car.

I smiled to myself in the backseat and touched the French braid my mom had done for me. Dad. Trying his "subtle" approach! "Oh, I don't know . . . ," I replied breezily. "I haven't been hanging out with them much. I'm too busy with Ricky and his cool friends." I caught the slight, barely perceptible anxious glance that passed between my parents and tried to pretend I hadn't noticed it. But secretly I felt good.

In a guilty kind of way.

Lately I'd begun to realize that my parents thought *much* more was going on between Ricky and me than was really happening at all. And the more I inflamed their concern, the more attention I got. Like today. No way we would be going on a family picnic if my parents weren't worried I was being "influenced" by the "wrong element" (or whatever they called guys with tattoos and leather!).

"Honey, you really shouldn't lose sight of your old crowd," Mom chimed in as I picked at the flaking goth-black nail polish I was wearing. "I know you're experimenting with a . . . uh . . . new *identity,* which means a new social circle," she yammered on. "But you know what they say: new friends are silver, but old friends are gold."

I said nothing in the backseat, although the guilt I felt about not being exactly truthful bubbled up through my insides. I knew I was being manipulative and milking the situation—trying to make out like there was really something romantic going on between Ricky and me. But I couldn't help myself from misleading my parents. Because the more I misled them, the more they seemed like *my* parents and not just the baby-to-be's.

Plus I wasn't lying when I told them I liked

spending time with Ricky. I did like it. A lot.

"Is, uh, Richard involved much in the school?" Dad asked stiffly at one point, and I shook my head firmly and snorted. *Richard! Maybe Ricky is his full name, Dad. Ever considered that?* Involved in the school! Going for the swim team or the Mathletes! It was a funny idea, and I giggled even thinking of it. Which prompted my mom to give up her delicate approach and just kick right in with a firm lecture about "getting off track" and "that *type* of guy."

"Oh, puh-leeze!" I rolled my eyes and stared out of the car window as my parents tried to make out like Ricky was the son of Satan. So he skipped a couple of classes and rode a motorcycle! Big deal.

But annoying as it was, I had to admit, this lecture had its bonus features: the more worried my parental unit was about Ricky, the more worried they were about me. And deceptive as it was, I couldn't help rolling along with it all. I know it was weak, but right there in the car, despite even the annoying comments about Ricky, I felt good. My parents still cared about me. And it was nice to know.

". . . I just hope you don't throw everything away, Joely," Mom blathered on, and I looked up, amazed to see we were already pulling up into our garage. She'd been lecturing me for, like, thirty minutes . . . and I'd barely heard a word. "Friends and grades should not come in second just because a boy pays you attention."

"Uh-huh," I murmured incomprehensibly as Mom continued on with her lecture. *God!* In a way,

I admired my mom. She could speak for hours when she got into a topic. Usually it was impressionism for her students at the community college. But now it happened to be Ricky.

Which had the opposite effect. I wanted to call him now more than ever. I'd only ever spoken to Ricky a couple of times on the phone before, but if I phoned now, it wouldn't be weird. After all, Carla was due any moment now, and I could always just say I wanted to check in for a stat report.

I told myself this even though my heart beat wildly during the time it took for me to dial Ricky's phone number from my bedroom extension. Why was my heart racing like that anyway? I got annoyed at myself for being stupid as Ricky's dad called him to the phone. I *was* only calling about Carla. So phoning was totally no biggie.

"Hey," I said, trying to sound nonchalant as Ricky picked up the phone.

"Hey, what's up?" He sounded a little rushed. A little annoyed, maybe. Maybe it was just my imagination.

"Is Carla doing okay?" I asked.

"Yeah," Ricky replied. "Mom and kid both doing well. His name is Marco. And he looks kind of like me. But cuter, if you like the scrunchy pink look."

"She *had* the baby?" I gripped the phone in surprise. Ricky and I had talked so much about Carla's pregnancy that the birth of her baby felt like a big deal to me personally. "Why didn't you call?" I blurted suddenly, and then cringed. But the truth was, I was a little disappointed. I'd felt sure Ricky would want to talk to me when the whole thing went down.

"But I did." Ricky sounded surprised and confused. "I called you on Friday and told your mom to give you an urgent message. I figured your not calling me back meant something."

Mom? Right then my heart began to slow into a hard beat of anger.

"Maybe your mom forgot," Ricky said generously.

"Yeah," I mumbled. "She must have. Because I never got the message. That's the truth, Ricky." But I knew my mom hadn't forgotten. An urgent message is an urgent message. And my mom is like an elephant, and I don't mean as in "big," I mean as in she *never* forgets.

"No big deal," Ricky said. "Oh, hey, I'd better go. My sister's calling me. Maybe she needs help with the baby or something."

And a couple of good-byes later, we'd hung up.

She forgot on purpose! The truth banged through my skull as I lay back on my bed. I knew my mother didn't approve of Ricky, but keeping phone calls from me? That was low. Really low.

Not to mention awkward. Ricky wasn't an idiot. He knew as well as I did that my mom had simply elected not to give his message to me.

Tears of anger glinted in my eyes, and I turned to roll on my side, reaching for my favorite feather pillow. And as I did so, I caught a flash of my own reflection in the mirror on my nightstand, a bit of my French braid turning as I moved. *I've always loved your long hair, honey.* My mom's words from earlier in the day flickered through my thoughts, and right then and there I knew what I would do.

Forget confronting her. She'd just say she's so sorry, she forgot, what with hormones and all.

Mom knew how to upset me; that was for sure. But I knew how to upset her too.

Four

Joely

"JUST CUT IT all off," I said to Coco, the hair-stylist, as Shelby, Catherine, and Melanie's jaws dropped like trapdoors. "All off," I added in a bold voice that totally was not the way I felt. "Like Demi Moore in *G.I Jane.*"

"A military buzz?" Coco snapped her gum and looked at me dubiously from under her pierced eyebrows. "Are you sure about this?"

"Completely."

"Joely. Get a grip!" Shelby broke in, grabbing me by the shoulders, her blue eyes glittering nervously and a skitter of panic causing the silver bracelets down her long arms to jangle. "You've never had your hair shorter than butt length. A *bob* would be a radical step for you!"

"Yeah, Joels," Catherine whispered. "Why don't you go to a bob first before you make such a huge leap?"

"A bob . . ." I smiled breezily at the consternation of my friends and then refocused my gaze on Coco's locks. Coco had a short, punky do. Lots of spikes. Gel. That kind of thing. Totally un-me, in other words. "Or maybe cut my hair like yours," I told her. "It's cool."

During this whole show I had what I think was an air of completely untypical laid-backness. And confidence. While my friends were wringing their hands and worrying that I was being rash in cutting off all my hair, worrying that I might regret the deed after it was done, I acted like I knew exactly what I was doing and was totally comfortable with it.

Not!

The truth of it was, I was terror stricken. Completely, totally a bundle of nerves. But I figured everyone was this way when they changed their look. That was what change was all about, right? Doing something you've never done before. Taking risks. And while it was true my friends' nerves were *so* not helping my own, I took a deep breath and plastered a cheery smile to my face as Coco led me to the basin for a shampoo. Of course my friends would act like this was the end of the world! Outrageous to them was a pair of purple flares from Urban Outfitters. My crowd was a preppy, carefully casual crowd, all three of them wearing J. Crew cargo pants that very moment!

But I'm not them. I told myself this over and over again, like it was my mantra, as Coco shampooed my hair briskly and the faces of Shelby and the others

64

loomed anxiously above my own. *I'm just trying to live a little!* I coached myself, picturing my new buzz cut or spike cut or Mohawk or whatever it was going to be. The image, however, terrified me even more. I did not have the attitude to carry off such a cut. I did not have the right face, the right clothes, the right personality!

Nonsense! my inner voice growled back at me. I set my jaw, determined to embrace the new me that would come out of this. Of course change was freaky, but maybe being hostile to it would only make it worse. *Make friends with it,* my brain chirped at me as Coco boxed my ears dry with a towel (or at least that's what it felt like). *Make friends with the new you!*

Huh? I shook my head to clear the weird junk that seemed to be rolling around in there. See? This was what happened when I started to panic. But a few deep breaths and I would be fine. Ready to go.

"Do you think maybe you're trying to impress someone with this haircut, Joely?" Shelby piped up a little nervously. "Don't bite my head off or anything," she added as my eyes narrowed dangerously.

Why can't she keep her stupid ideas to herself? I thought angrily. But I knew the answer to that. Shelby always spoke her mind, no matter what. It was one of the things about her I had admired most. Before she made *me* the object of her observations!

"I am not *trying* to do anything! I just want a haircut. So don't have a cow," I shot back, but I was unsettled by Shelby's remark and squirmed a little as I gazed at my reflection in the mirror. But I was. I was trying

65

to hurt my mom. And that wasn't cool, even if she'd hurt me by "forgetting" about Ricky's urgent call.

Maybe this wasn't about my mom at all. Maybe I was trying to impress Ricky with this cut.

No way! If anything, this cut was about upsetting my mom. That was the original idea. But thinking of Mom only increased my panicky state of mind. She would *flip her lid* when she saw me! Not that I didn't have my speech all planned. And what could Mom say anyway? It's not like she hadn't changed a few things about her appearance (try the big, moon-shaped belly, for one thing)!

But as Coco wiped down her scissors and the straight razor with which she would be spiking my hair, I couldn't help biting down hard on my lip, almost to the point of breaking the skin. Cutting off all my hair *was* a big deal for me. My friends were right. And Shelby was also at least partially right in suspecting that Ricky somehow had something to do with this. It was true, he had influenced my new look. And could I deny that I liked his compliments on my wardrobe and makeup?

Either way, change is good, I told myself, trying to relax although my hands gripped the armrests of the barber's chair, my nails digging into the leather like eagle's claws. I took deep breaths, in and out, as the scissors edged in, closer . . . closer. . . . *Who cares why you're doing it . . . just do it. . . .* Closer . . . closer . . . *just do it, just do it, just—*

"Stop!" I yelled, just as the scissors began their first, tiny snip.

"What?" Coco and I both stared at my terrified mug in the mirror.

"I can't go through with it." There. I'd said it. My long locks would be saved, and I would get to go home feeling like a chicken. Or feeling like myself, just a hair (and I mean that literally!) away from becoming someone else.

"Thank goodness!" Shelby breathed a sigh of relief as Coco shrugged and began to trim the usual quarter inch from the bottom of my hair.

But I wasn't smiling. Because I wasn't that happy about my decision, even though I knew it was the right one. *What does this mean?* I asked myself, staring at my reflection. Was I too conventional and boring to be on the edge? You see, in my heart of hearts I guess I knew that this whole hair thing had something to do with wanting Ricky to think I was cool. Shelby was (annoyingly) right about that. Now that Carla had had her baby, I hadn't seen much of Ricky. I kept telling myself he was busy with helping out, but I wasn't sure about that at all. So maybe subconsciously I felt he would ignore me from now on unless I did something to convince him that I was still worth his time.

But I'd caved. I hadn't gotten the radical new look I'd come for, which proved something. Although I couldn't quite figure out what. Was I really just a boring Goody Two-shoes? I didn't know the answer to that, but I knew one thing for sure: Ricky and I were different. There was no getting around that one.

But were we *too* different to be friends?
I knew a good way to find out.

Ricky

Dingdong!

I jiggled my foot nervously as the doorbell sounded through Joely's house. Make that her mansion. Well, maybe that's exaggerating, but the big house with the pillared entryway sure beat the sight of the Lenci single-story "ranch" home.

Why was I nervous? I wondered about this as I waited for Joely to come to the door. It wasn't the possibility of seeing her folks that made me feel wigged out. I knew they were both working this evening. That was why Joely had asked me over, I guess, and I'd said I might stop by on my way to the Roxy bar, where I shoot pool with the guys. But . . . I don't know. Maybe it was the big house that made me feel weird and the fact that Joely and I had never hung out except for at school, unless you counted that ten-minute time at the mall and the five-minute whirl around the school parking lot.

"Hey," I said as Joely flung open the door.

"Hey! Come on in."

I shot her a smile. "You look nice."

She did look nice because she's a nice-looking girl, but I was mostly just being polite. The fact is, Joely's got this new look going on: black leather, heavy-duty mascara. And I noticed she even had on a leather spike bracelet. Deena has one of those. But on Joely it looked a bit strange, and secretly I preferred the way she used to look.

Joely didn't need all of that heavy stuff to look pretty. She's naturally pretty and always had great style, a lot of color in her wardrobe, real natural in the makeup department. But I could tell she liked the compliment I gave her, so I knew I was saying the right thing, which is very important around girls and often hard to do. "Cool bracelet," I added, and she blushed.

"Glad you could stop by," Joely said as we headed for the den, me worried my boots might scuff the fancy hardwood floors.

"Yeah. I can hang for a bit," I told her as I walked through the kitchen and tried not to ogle. If my pop could see the marble-topped counters and smooth cabinetwork . . . *wow!* "So . . . nice place," I said as I sat down on a leather sofa in the den. Joely had popcorn happening and some movie on the tube.

"It's okay." Joely shrugged, and I wondered if she had any idea how huge and nice her home really was. *These rich kids,* I couldn't help thinking as I looked around at all the custom-made bookshelves and expensive-looking paintings. *They don't know what they've got!*

"So what are you watching?" I asked Joely, to make conversation.

"Old movies. I just put in *West Side Story.* Want to watch?"

We sat for a few moments, and was it my imagination, or was the movie kind of embarrassing us both? It sure embarrassed me. All that stuff about who should date who and who was from which side of town . . . I squirmed a little on the couch. And Joely looked awkward herself, although I was trying hard not to look her way at all.

"So . . . want a soda?" Joely asked suddenly, pausing the movie.

"I got a better idea." I grinned and lifted up my jacket to reveal the six-pack I'd stashed under my arm. A beer with Joely might be a good thing. Maybe we'd both relax a little, because it was obvious we both felt a tad strange, seeing the other out of school. Like, *socially*.

"Oh!" Joely's eyes widened as she locked onto the Budweiser, and she looked suddenly pale and kind of . . . terrified. "No thanks." She covered quickly with a smile. "I mean, you go ahead, but I, uh, better not. I mean, I usually would," she added. "But I probably shouldn't in my own house, with my parents coming home later . . . you know?"

"Yeah." I nodded. But I knew that wasn't the truth of it. I could tell by the look on her face that what she was really saying was that she wasn't into drinking. Which was completely cool and all. I had no problem with that. I just wished she would be honest with me.

"But you go ahead." Joely jerked her head in the direction of the six-pack I'd put on the coffee table.

"That's okay."

For what felt like the longest time there was a silence. Just the ticking of some old clock—no doubt a family heirloom or something—and the sound of our own breathing. It was really uncomfortable in there. And suddenly I wished I hadn't come over at all. Joely obviously thought I was some drunk, and I felt kind of annoyed that she felt she had to act like she was down with drinking when clearly that wasn't her style. Honesty is what I like. People who are straight up and comfortable with who they are.

Why can't things just be simple? I wondered. And then I remembered one way to make them simple. "How about a little Frankie Blue Eyes?" I suggested, and instantly Joely's face lit up.

"My parents have it all on vinyl," she said as we made our way over to the stereo.

And right then the evening loosened up and took a different turn. Joely's old man had this huge collection of old music, and some of those albums were really rare. So we sat and listened to music, to great old Sinatra standards like "New York, New York" and to old Rat Pack show tunes I'd never even heard.

"This is a gold mine," I murmured to Joely as we flipped through the albums. She smiled at me, her face totally relaxed and happy looking, and I knew then that everything was cool between us. We were still buddies. It didn't matter that she lived up on the hill and I was just some Italian kid from down the way. We were just two people talking and getting along. The way it should be.

"'I recall . . . Central Park in fall,'" Joely sang along while I bust my gut laughing, although I have to admit, she looked very cute sitting there pretending to be the man, Mr. Sinatra himself.

"Are you insulting my musical gifts?" Joely shot back, and punched me on the arm, acting like she was all hurt.

"I say stick with math, Carmichael," I kidded her back, and then we both cracked up until suddenly Joely looked panicked.

"What's up?"

"The garage door," she murmured nervously. "I can hear it. Guess my mom decided to come home early after all."

"Well, I have to get moving myself," I said smoothly, getting up to retrieve the six-pack from the coffee table.

"I'm not trying to hustle you out of here or anything," Joely blabbed anxiously. "It's just the . . . alcohol . . . and everything," she finished lamely as she scuttled me toward the front door.

"Sure. Later." I held up the six-pack and then backed out the door and down over the lawn. As I gunned my bike, I looked up to see her face, and she gave me a nervous wave before closing the door behind her.

Close call. I sat there in the dark of the driveway and then revved the engine of my Harley and took off. It *was* a close call. But I knew that Joely hadn't hustled me out because of the six-pack. That stuff can be hidden faster than getting a guy out of the house. What she was really trying to avoid was having me face-to-face with her folks again.

And to be honest, I wasn't exactly hot for a run-in with her mom myself. The woman who "forgot" my urgent message. To me, that was old news, so I hadn't brought it up, and I was glad Joely hadn't either. Like we needed another reminder that we weren't exactly *similar?*

So, all in all, it was a good thing I'd gotten out of there fast. But no matter how many times I told myself I didn't care about the way the evening ended, I felt angry. I knew I was Joely's parents' worst nightmare, and I knew she knew it. And although that's the kind of thing my friends would laugh about and maybe even think was kind of cool, it got me the wrong way.

Snobs, I thought angrily as I veered down the hill and out onto the road.

Be cool, I told myself as I cruised toward downtown. *You shouldn't have brought the beer, and you know it.*

So what were you trying to prove? I asked myself.

Maybe that the Lencis and the Carmichaels have nothing in common. And you proved that, all right.

Forget it, man. A game of pool would take the edge off. . . . *So chill!*

But that was easier said than done, and instead of cooling off I gunned the engine and picked up more speed than I knew was good for me. I'd been doing that a lot lately, and although I knew it wasn't safe, it helped me feel the way I needed to feel: like nothing's in my way and Edenvale was just someplace I was passing through on my way to someplace better.

Ricky

"Your shot." Jake stepped back so I could get a better angle on the cue ball. It was an easy shot, and I'd have no trouble sinking the ball. I needed the victory too. I usually ace the nightly pool games at the Roxy bar.

"Damn!" I swore under my breath as the white ball bounced off the green felt without even skimming the black.

"Bad luck," a voice said in my ear, and I looked up to see Coco shooting me her cool, slightly mean signature smirk. That's Coco's version of a smile.

"Hey, Coco," I replied, thanking her as she passed me a beer. It had been a long time since I'd seen Coco. She was that type of girl. Sometimes she was around. Sometimes she wasn't. And most of the time I was on the lookout for her. We all were. Because Coco's eighteen, and she's one of the coolest chicks there is. Rides a motorcycle like it's do or die. Cuts crazy, inspired punked-out hairstyles. Plays a mean game of pool.

Used to be my girlfriend.

Well, sort of. Coco doesn't belong to anyone.

"So what you been up to lately, soldier?" Coco teased, pulling a box of cigarettes from her leather jacket pocket. Instantly both Jake and Andy were at her side, holding out their Zippos. Everyone wanted to be near Coco.

"Not much," I said, straightening up and leaning on my pool cue. "My sis had a kid. So I've been dealing with that."

"Got a light?" Coco said, ignoring the other guys.

"Sure." I was surprised as I fumbled in my jacket for matches. Surprised but definitely pleased that Coco seemed to want my time. Lately she had been ignoring me and hanging around some older guy called Rod Someone-or-other. . . . But now she seemed to only be interested in talking to me.

"So . . . seeing anyone? Any crushes on any classmates?" Coco teased as she fixed me with her big blue eyes, rimmed in dark black. She'd dropped out of school last year.

"Huh?" I couldn't pick up what she was driving at, so I just shrugged. But Jake and Andy seemed ready to answer for me.

"Yeah, Rick Man here's got quite the social life happening," Jake said to Coco with a grin.

"Very *uptown*," Andy chimed in, put his nose in the air imitating a snob, and then everyone laughed. Except me.

"What the hell is that supposed to mean?" I said, annoyed to be the butt of the joke. I didn't appreciate all the sudden attention. And anyway, it wasn't true. Passing some time with Joely Carmichael did not make me some uptown guy.

"Keep out of my business," I added harshly as a fresh round of laughter rippled through the group.

"C'mon, Ricky," Coco purred, her hand on the collar of my jacket, but I pulled away roughly. I was bugged. I was angry. I knew my friends were only trying to get a rise out of me, but I was not in the mood for it. And as Coco stared me down, I looked away and headed for the jukebox.

But not before I caught Coco's look: *What is wrong with you?* her eyes said. She was as surprised as I was that I wasn't hanging on her every word. I mean, I used to go out with Coco. Hell, I was crazy about her. Everyone was. *But not anymore.*

I knew it as I looked at her and I knew it as I looked away. Something in me had changed. And it was downright out of character.

What was going on?

Five

Joely

"EXCUSES DON'T HELP," Mom contended, piercing me with her sternest look as the nurse rubbed some gel on her belly. "Slacking off is slacking off, and whatever else is going on, your grades *always* take top priority. . . ."

"Do you believe this?" I murmured to Dad as Mom continued her speech despite the fact that we were in St. Stevens hospital and she was about to have another ultrasound. Because my mother is old for having a baby, extra precautions were being taken. Apparently it was important to verify "placental position," whatever that is, and fetal growth. Yet my mom seemed more worried about my (only marginally) slipping grades and Ricky's influence than what was going on around her. Or *inside* her, for that matter!

"Dear, try to relax," Dad murmured to Mom as

she sat up on her elbows to try to make her point. "It doesn't help the baby, getting all fired up."

"Oh, Dennis," Mom snapped back. "The baby will be fine. But you know as well as I do that Joely's grades are sliding, and these things count!" She pointed a warning finger at me. "Colleges look at your junior-year results, young lady! Especially colleges like Princeton!"

Mom continued her diatribe on how I was changing, stopping only when the nurse finally whipped out something shaped like a soap bar and began moving it across Mom's belly.

"Mrs. Carmichael, if you could please take a deep breath," the nurse interrupted just as Mom got ready to launch into another lecture.

Thank God! The voice of Medical Reason! I thought, folding my arms and looking away, out the window, wishing I were anywhere but here. *Why am I even here?* I asked myself irritably. The answer was simple enough: my parents had practically forced me to go. This was a family thing, and it would be "nice to have you there," my dad had said. And so, reluctantly, I had come to this family thing. Only to have my parents once again arguing with me! So much for family bonding! They didn't even appreciate that I had taken time out from my life to be here, supporting Mom!

My head full of angry thoughts, I tried to space, attempting to block out the scene by counting how many SUVs there were in the parking lot outside. But after a moment my curiosity got the better of me. The nurse was saying something about the baby's position and how everything looked good. Relief flooded through me at that moment, and I even shared a smile with my dad. Not that I had yet forgiven him for bolstering Mom during the half-hour lecture I had just received, but . . . at least everything was okay, medically speaking.

And like I said, curiosity got the better of me when they started oohing and cooing at the monitor in front of the bed.

"Joely, look!" Mom murmured. And for a moment we all forgot where we had been and looked. There, on the screen in front of us all, was the baby.

I swallowed hard. I don't know what I had been imagining, but I hadn't quite pictured the baby to be so fully formed . . . and actually moving! You could even see one of its little hands opening and closing. "Is it sucking its thumb?" I asked incredulously as I saw the other hand closed in a fist near the baby's jaw.

"It's very common to see," the nurse replied, smiling as we all leaned in for a closer look.

"And listen!" Mom crowed, holding up this little handheld device to Dad. "You can hear the heartbeat!"

As Dad passed the device to me, I felt the strangest feeling. Something like excitement . . . or maybe just plain wonder. The baby's heartbeat was so strong, and it was cool to think you could actually listen in on a new life inside someone else.

"Wow," I murmured, and looked at both Mom

and Dad. Not even I could suppress a smile, and Mom's eyes were shining so brightly, it was as if we hadn't even argued at all that day. Like everything else had been wiped out and nothing existed but this happy moment.

Not that *I* was happy. I mean, if anything, the baby thing was just making me more nervous. Now that I could actually see him/her, I could no longer even hope to deny the reality that lay ahead. All the responsibilities I would have to face, all the traumas that lay just around the corner . . .

"Would you like to know the baby's gender?" the nurse asked my parents.

Mom looked at Dad, and then without hesitation she shook her head. "No. I think we'd like it to be a surprise," she said with a smile.

And right then the bubble of happiness I had felt popped. A surprise? I folded my arms and silently slipped out of the room, shaking my head in annoyance. *Haven't we all had enough surprises already?* I wondered, listening to the joyful murmurings of my baby-struck parents from inside the examination room.

And as I stood in the long, white corridor, I felt my stomach sink. Maybe it was the stark white walls and all those horrible fluorescent lights, or maybe it was the fact that my parents didn't even appear to have noticed my leaving. Whatever it was, I suddenly felt lonelier than I ever had before.

Everything felt weird too, sort of upside down or back to front, like I was living in a parallel universe, where nothing was quite what it seemed and everything was the opposite of what it should be. My feelings too seemed all mixed up. And for a moment I felt like I didn't even know who I was anymore. On the one hand, the ultrasound was kind of cool. But I still hated the whole baby thing . . . didn't I?

I just didn't know anymore.

"Joely?" my dad called from the doorway, but I slipped around a pillar so he couldn't see me. I needed to be alone. I needed to sort myself out.

So much was bothering me right then, I couldn't even really formulate it into proper order. But it went something like this: I couldn't deny that the baby bugged me and my parents' baby obsession bugged me even more. Yet it was obvious that the baby always saved my hide. When my parents were most mad—like a few minutes ago—the baby would distract them. And if it weren't for the baby, I wouldn't have ever spoken to Ricky. Which meant I ought to feel kind of glad about the baby situation. And maybe I even did. But somehow I just couldn't tell. I was so alienated from my own feelings, I felt like I couldn't even separate them out, couldn't work out the difference between love and hate, happiness and dread. . . .

Get a grip! I ordered myself, trying to summon the old me, the sensible, *coping* me. I needed that me. Not this other me, whose feelings somersaulted over each other without warning, whose emotions went from excitement to anger so fast, it made me seasick. I *had* to keep my head! There were only a few months left of calm before the storm. And if I spent the whole time worrying about the future, I wouldn't be able to hold on to the present.

Which meant I wouldn't enjoy that last chunk of time I had to be the only child in the family.

Keep your cool, I ordered myself as I stepped out from behind the pillar and got ready to join my parents. I still didn't feel ready to be with them, but on the other hand, I wanted to make the most of having them to myself. There was one indisputable fact in this whole sorry mess: the clock was ticking, and my solo time was almost up.

So work it as much as you can, I told myself. And by that I meant getting the conversations back onto me. Because even though Mom's lectures were a pain to listen to and Dad's worried expression got tedious after a while, I still preferred they be fixated on my "changes for the worse" than on you know who.

Ricky

"Wave to Mommy, little guy," I said to Marco as I steered the baby carriage past Lenci's on Main, the family restaurant. Of course the kid isn't nearly old enough to wave to Carla, but you never know. He could be a prodigy and surprise us all.

As I wheeled Marco down Main Street for his afternoon walk, I admit I felt like a goofball.

Marco's stroller is all baby blue with little teddy bears on it. Kind of embarrassing. Especially when three cute girls happened to be walking nearby.

I cringed as the three beauties (two brunettes and a blonde) neared me. How can a guy look suave and maintain his image when he's pushing a baby around? But what could I do?

The girls drew nearer, and then almost at the same time, their faces lit up like lightbulbs.

"Omigod," the blonde squealed. "What an adorable baby!"

"Hey, there, cutie," one of the brunettes chimed in, and I had to stop while they squealed and fell all over the carriage.

What is it with women and mushy talk? Even Carla, of all people, does it. It must be some genetic thing, but they just seem to naturally start doing the *ga-ga-goo-goo* talk when they get near a baby. Not me, though. I talk to Marco like he's a person. That way when he gets to be one, it won't be such a shock.

"He's so beautiful," the blonde said to me as the other two continued to smother the baby with their admiration. "You must be so proud," she added with a sexy smile.

Immediately I felt totally flustered. "He's not . . . he's not mine!" I spluttered. "I'm the uncle," I added in a more normal tone of voice.

"Okay . . ." The blonde looked at me way different now. She had real pretty brown eyes, and they flickered with interest. "Well, it sure is nice of you to walk your nephew. I don't know a lot of guys who would do that."

"Thanks," I muttered casually, but inside I felt suddenly pretty good, and as the girls waved me good-bye, looking at me in a flirty way, I grinned to myself.

"Thanks, Marco," I said to the little guy. Who'd have thought it—a baby as a girl magnet? Then on second thought I realized it made a lot of sense. Girls like to see that a guy can be all sensitive and strong at the same time.

"So young and you're already a pro at getting babes," I said to Marco as I turned the corner and headed back to the restaurant. "Who knows," I added. "Maybe you'll be like James Dean. All those screaming women . . . fame and fortune . . . dividing your time between New York and LA and Paris . . ."

I could feel more eyes on me as we passed Café Colonial, which was just a block from Lenci's. I turned my head and caught the glances of more girls. It seemed like they were everywhere. I admit, Marco is a good-looking guy. But I liked to also think that some of the admiring looks were going out to me, for walking a baby and looking like I was having fun doing it.

"Thanks for the walk," I said to Marco as we neared the restaurant. "I had fun." And as I picked Marco out of the stroller and headed inside, I realized it *had* been really fun. A lot more fun than I would have thought. And for the first time since

Marco was born, I realized that there were some pretty okay things about having a baby in the family. In between the crying and the diaper changing and all that stuff, there were some halfway decent moments.

Joely should know this, I thought suddenly, out of the blue. I hadn't seen Joely in a while, what with Marco and all the new stuff happening. But right then I realized how I could make her life a little easier. I knew where she was, emotionally, right now. I'd been there. Her mom was maybe three months away from giving birth, and Joely was probably freaked out of her skull.

"Did you have a good time?" Ma asked me as she took Marco from me in the kitchen of the restaurant.

"Yeah," I added, and smiled at her. "I did."

And that's when I picked up the phone. Whether she liked it or not, Joely's baby bro or sis was soon to make an appearance. So the way I figured, she might as well get some practice with the real thing . . . and see that it could be fun.

Joely

"Thank you, Mrs. Lenci," I said as Ricky's mom handed me a glass of iced tea. "It's delicious," I added, trying not to be nervous even though I could feel Carla watching me.

I had been so excited when Ricky had called and

invited me over to baby-sit with him. I mean, I wasn't excited to baby-sit, exactly, but . . . you know what I mean.

And Ricky's family were supernice! His mom and dad were the kind of people you instantly felt comfortable with. Really warm and easygoing. But Carla was a bit scary. I could tell she didn't like me right from the moment Ricky introduced us and she barked her hello to me like I had just said something nasty to her.

Or maybe she's just like that. Maybe all new mothers are like that! I didn't know, but I sure hoped not.

"Ma, could you just get the formula already?" Carla snipped from the couch as her mother bustled into the kitchen. "And Ricky, wipe that grease stain off your hands before you pick up my child!"

Yikes! I tried to cover the alarm that sprang into my widening eyes, but the situation really was starting to bother me. Carla obviously called the shots in the house. And I started to wonder what Mom would be like when "Chloe" was born. Would she also order me and Dad around like we were her servants?

"See you later," Mrs. Lenci said as she gathered her handbag and shuffled Mr. Lenci and Carla out of the house. "And if you're hungry, Joely—"

"Ma, we get it! Lasagna and apple pie in the fridge," Ricky said teasingly. "Now get to the restaurant, would you?"

"Don't mess up the feeding times," Carla

barked at Ricky, shaking her head of glamorous curls as if he'd already messed up the feeds. "Don't screw it up!" she added before her face softened for the first time all afternoon, and she bent to give Marco a kiss.

"I just ignore her," Ricky explained cheerfully as the door slammed shut. "As you can see, Carla *really* needs a break."

I smiled, and Marco gurgled at me. He'd just had his bottle, and instead of the screaming brat I'd expected, he was all smiley, even when Ricky juggled him up and down to burp him.

"He's cute," I said, reaching out to touch his peach-fuzz head. He was cute. As long as I didn't have to hold him. I wouldn't know what to do with a baby. I'd probably make him cry. But Ricky sure seemed to know his way around it all. He was like an expert, walking up and down with the baby over his shoulder, rubbing his back so he wouldn't get indigestion.

And I had to admit, Ricky kind of suited the whole baby thing. Somehow looking at him with a baby in his arms made him even hotter than he already was. *He's going to make a great dad,* I thought as I sipped my tea.

"What're you thinking, Carmichael?" Ricky caught me off guard, and I struggled to look unflustered. "You looked really far away for a moment," he said.

"I guess." I smiled and shifted uncomfortably on the couch, trying not to blush and give away the fact that I was thinking of Ricky. Too late. My face burned a deep shade of pink, and I was mortified. And angry with myself. This was supposed to be an afternoon of "Baby 101." That's why Ricky had called. To help me get prepared.

"Seriously, what are you thinking?" Ricky probed, cocking his head. "I can see you've got something on your mind."

"Actually, I was totally spacing." I tried to cover up. "Thinking about nothing. I do that some-times." *Idiot!* Listening to myself, I felt like such a moron. But what was I supposed to say?

And why are you even thinking about Ricky when you should be watching him and picking up tips! I chided myself, wishing I had more self-control. It was such a waste of time to even think about Ricky, except as a friend who could help me learn about coping with babies. I knew Ricky would never feel anything for me except platonic friend-ship, yet I couldn't help it. Despite the obvious fact that I was so obviously not his type and would never be dangerous enough/cool enough for him, I still caught myself thinking about him in ways that were not . . . well . . . *useful.*

"So, um . . ." I cleared my throat and took a long slug of the cool tea in an attempt to chill the blush burning my cheeks. "So I, uh, can see you've got the holding-and-feeding thing down," I stam-mered as Ricky came and sat down next to me after placing Marco in the bassinet next to the couch for his postlunch nap.

"Yeah. I got it." Ricky smiled, and I felt his eyes kind of staring at me.

Help! I took another extra-big gulp of tea to keep my face color-free, but I could feel Ricky's eyes on me. Staring.

"What?" I said finally.

"I, uh, sorry." Ricky looked away and then smiled sheepishly. "I didn't mean to stare. It's just your . . . eyes look so dramatic with that makeup thing you got going on."

"Really?" I squeaked, unable to suppress the fluttery-warm feeling in my stomach—like I'd just swallowed a firefly. . . .

"It's cool," Ricky added, fixing me with his amazing green eyes and causing me to wonder why it is that guys always have longer eyelashes than girls when it's the girls who really want them.

"But it kind of gets in the way," Ricky added. Suddenly the firefly feeling was gone, and I felt self-conscious. Had I put my makeup on wrong? Did Ricky think I looked stupid and he was just trying to say it nicely?

"Don't get me wrong," Ricky filled in quickly as my eyes fell to my lap. "You could pull off any look. But I always liked the way you used to look. You always had your own, totally original style. Like that red dress you used to wear. I really liked that. Now all you wear is black."

"You remember my dress?" I blurted, even though that was just the kind of obvious thing I didn't need to say. But I was shocked! I would never in a million years have thought that Ricky of all people kept tabs on what I wore. But the fact that he did made me feel important. Flattered. Shaky at the knees.

"I thought you liked black," I said quietly, feeling suddenly shy around Ricky.

"I do." He smiled and jerked a thumb toward his chest, clad in a black T-shirt (and filling it out extremely well). "I wear a lot of black . . . but that's me. You look really good in red. And also in that green color you used to wear a lot."

Was I imagining it, or did Ricky look shy now?

Suddenly there was a silence in the room. Neither of us said anything; we just kind of smiled at each other. That was when my heart suddenly picked up an extra sixty beats a second, and I felt weirdly light-headed. In a good kind of way. *He thinks I have original style!* I gloated, still trying to grasp what I'd heard. There I was, trying to be cooler in smudgy kohl eye makeup and black outfits, when all along Ricky had liked me the way I was! It seemed a bit too good to be true. But he'd said it, and if there was one thing I'd picked up about Ricky, it was that he always spoke his mind.

Thank the Pope I didn't punk out my hair! I breathed a sigh of relief, still riding high on a bubble of Ricky's flattery, feeling another blush wave warming my face but not even caring this time. Because Ricky himself looked kind of self-conscious, although he had edged closer to me on the couch.

And right then our eyes met. Really met. Not just

like when you look at someone, but like when you look *into* someone and your eyes are locked together. Ricky leaned in a little closer toward me, and that's when the fireflies came back: a million of them, flickering up and down my spine. His eyes were so intense, as if he was seeing me for the first time.

Is he going to kiss me?

I *had* to be kidding myself. But he *was* moving closer toward me, and like a magnet, I was moving closer toward him without even trying.

Our arms brushed. An electric shock jolted right through me, melting my insides with its force, and at that point I lost all ability to even puzzle out why a guy like Ricky would be kissing me, of all people, because I knew it was going to happen, and that was all that counted.

I closed my eyes as Ricky's hand slightly touched the outside of my own. My heart was all I could hear, just the sound of my own, thumping—

Waaaaa!

That's when even my gong of a heart was drowned out by this awful, piercing, car-alarm wail. Except that it wasn't a car alarm and couldn't be turned off with a key. It was the baby.

Instantly Ricky sprang up from the couch as if it were on fire and went to pick up Marco. As for me, I didn't know what to do. But I knew the moment was over. And now that it was over, I began to doubt it had ever even happened in the first place. Ricky about to kiss *me?*

Dream on, Joely!

Six

Ricky

"**M**AN, WE SHOULD just cut class and hit the road," Jake grumbled as he slammed his locker. "It's so *warm* out," he added, peering longingly out of the school-hall windows. "We should be riding."

Jake was right, of course. Sitting in a classroom trying to fake like you even cared seemed so dumb when you could be out on the open road, faking nothing and doing what you loved. But I had a good reason for wanting to be at school right now. There were only a few weeks left until summer vacation, and I knew that once summer began, Joely and I probably wouldn't see much of each other. We ran in different crowds; plus her mom would be having the baby soon, and like it or not, Joely would have to be involved. There was only a small window of vacation time for Joely . . . and that was when she'd be heading to Chicago for her Mathletics competition (or whatever the heck it was called). So you see, I knew we'd be going our separate ways soon. And I wasn't sure I wanted to yet.

I was thinking all of those thoughts. And right then, that's when she showed up.

"Hey!" I waved at Joely as she came down the corridor toward me. She was walking with Shelby and some of the other Squeaky Cleans, but she looked great as she smiled at me. I noticed immediately that she'd gone back to her old look. Blue halter top, those capri pants all the girls are wearing these days . . . she looked really cute. So much better than Rocker Chick Joely. Somehow that just wasn't *her*.

"Let's go already." Jake interrupted my thoughts, jerking his head in the direction of the exit sign marking the stairs at the end of the corridor. But I shook my head.

"You go. I'll see you later."

Jake cocked his head, but I wasn't giving him any details. "Whatever, man," he said finally, and sloped off.

I could see Jake was confused by me, and in a way, so was I. When I first started hanging out with Joely, I never thought anything would ever happen between us, except as friends. The reasons are obvious enough. . . .

But sometimes logic just doesn't seem reasonable. Or else you think you got it all worked out, but then the weirdest little moments can happen, which totally mess with your mind: like last month, when Joely and I almost kissed. If Marco hadn't ruined the moment by screaming for a diaper change, I'm pretty sure we would have kissed. At least, I liked to think she wanted to. But I didn't know for sure.

So find out! A part of me really wanted to push this thing, and as Joely neared the lockers, I felt suddenly ready to just go for it. Ask her out. See what it would be like to go out with her on a date. Figure out once and for all if anything was there between us or if I was just picking up false signals.

"Hey, Ricky." Joely's voice was a little softer (shyer?) than usual. Not really her chirpy self. I think she also felt kind of awkward about that moment back at my place. Because right after that, we just acted like nothing had happened, although I think we both felt like some chemistry was happening.

Only one way to know . . . I walked over to Joely's locker. But although asking a girl out usually isn't a big deal to me, as I got closer to Joely, I suddenly couldn't do it.

Problem is, since our "moment," things haven't been the same between Joely and me. I know on my side I've been feeling kind of caught: wanting to talk to her but then also figuring we should take the baby crying as a sign that we weren't meant to kiss. That we needed to keep our distance. So although we've been going through the motions of being cool to each other, things have been kind of strained. Like right now.

"So what's happening?" I said to Joely, trying to

look relaxed even though I was still fifty-fifty on the date thing and stressing big time.

"Nothing much." Joely's expression was hard to read as she swooped down toward her books, her long hair shading her face.

"School's almost done," I said, feeling immediately like a moron for stating the obvious.

"Yup." Joely stood up then and turned to face me, flashing me a smile that looked, I don't know, a little forced? *Or maybe you're imagining it.* Maybe nothing was wrong between me and Joely, and maybe I should just smile back, walk away, and drop all of those other ideas about going on dates and looking for something more.

But then there's that other side of the coin: you know, the nothing-ventured-nothing-gained side.

"So . . . any end-of-year parties going down?" I asked Joely, trying to tune out her giggly girl posse, who were standing off to the side, whispering and generally acting about as uncool as they were.

"None that you'd be into going to," Joely replied with a little laugh, and I laughed too. She was right, and somehow we both started cracking up, probably each of us picturing the other trying to fit in at the other's friends' parties. Me drinking pop with Shelby and playing Trivial Pursuit. Joely in over her head at some bar, trying to deal with the sleaze factor from the other side of town.

But right then, as I looked at Joely, I could see that no matter what our differences were, we still connected in some way. I know it sounds corny, but that's the truth. And as we stood there, I knew I wanted to figure out if there was something more to that connection.

So I looked her straight in the eye, took a breath, and said it. "Would you like to go out with me?"

Joely's eyes widened in surprise. I could see I'd caught her totally off guard, and she was obviously still trying to figure out what I meant. "Like on a . . . ?"

"—date," I finished firmly. "Yeah. Dinner or something."

That's when her eyes lit up, got all shiny. I couldn't tell if she was excited or panicked or awkward or all three. And suddenly I worried that I'd done the wrong thing by asking her out. Freaked her out or something. So I shoved my hands in my pockets. I mean, it's not a big deal. A date *is* just a date. It's not like a marriage proposal.

"When?" Joely replied in a businesslike way. She pulled out her agenda book and a pen, still looking flustered but doing a good job of concealing whatever she felt about what I'd asked.

"Next Friday?"

"Okay. Yes. That would be nice."

"Good."

Now I was out of words, and we both were going to be late—Joely for class and me for a ride with Jake. But as we separated, I felt that some of the awkwardness of the moment was still with me. A date was no big deal, but it still had its expectations. I had asked her, but what if we didn't gel on our night out? Would the buddy vibe between us be ruined then? Had I made a mistake by even doing this?

As my ma would say, "Only time will tell."

Joely

"Fresh pesto pasta à la Joely, coming up!" I announced, beaming such a huge smile at my mom that my cheeks felt like they might crack. "Anything else you feel like?" I added as I chopped enthusiastically at the fresh basil.

"Sounds wonderful, honey," my mom replied as she waddled up to take a look. "Goodness . . . there's enough pesto here to feed the whole county."

I looked down at the chopping board in front of me and realized she was right. I had been so busy grinning and daydreaming about my date with Ricky that I'd practically decimated Dad's entire herb garden.

Date with Ricky. The words still sounded weird and fresh and exciting. I'd been walking on air all day, ever since he'd asked me out at exactly 2:47 P.M. I couldn't stop smiling, and for once I was even going out of my way to make an extra-nice dinner, without making Mom feel bad for it!

I guess you could say I was on cloud nine.

"What *is* it with you?" Mom queried, elbowing me and flashing a quizzical smile. "You look like the cat that just ate the canary."

"Oh, it's nothing," I lied, keeping my eyes on

the blender in front of me and therefore far away from Mom's. I had a hard time lying to Mom. It was as if the woman could look right through me. And this time I didn't even want to lie. I was busting to tell the whole world what had happened. I had a real date. And not just with anyone. A date with Ricky Lenci.

I'd barely been on any dates before, and I'd certainly never been asked out by anyone nearly as cute or cool as Ricky. I was stunned. So stunned that all I could do was grin and chop and blend, like some kind of mad chef. For once all my fears about the baby were suspended too. Mom had only nine weeks to go, but I'd put my worries about her and the baby on hold. I was happy. Happy and secretive.

But Mom wasn't buying my silence, and as she plopped down at the kitchen table, I could feel her curiosity wafting across to me like some kind of supernatural vapor. Powerful. Hard to resist.

"Okay, I do have something," I blurted finally, looking up at Mom. A part of me knew I shouldn't say too much about it, but another part of me knew that even if Mom disapproved of Ricky, she would surely relate to my excitement. Mom is a romantic person after all, and she and I had spent many hours watching the Romantic Classics channel together. That should count for something, right?

"I have a dinner date with Ricky. Next Friday." My eyes felt like they had bits of glitter stuck in them. I could feel them shining, and my stomach still felt weirdly floaty, the way it had felt when

Ricky first surprised me by asking me out. "I'm pretty psyched," I finished with a grin, looking at Mom for a reaction.

Her face fell.

Instantly I dropped from cloud nine to cloud seven.

"What's the problem?" I demanded coldly as Mom shook her head and sighed. "I'm allowed to date, aren't I?"

Mom leveled her gaze at me and then ran a tired hand through her corkscrew curls. "Yes, you are, Joely," she said evenly. "You are allowed to date. If the person is appropriate for you."

I reddened in anger and gave the blender a few hard pulses while I tried to swallow Mom's words. What did she know about who was appropriate for me? That should be my decision, not hers! "You know nothing about Ricky," I shot back. "You're just prejudiced against him because he's from a different part of town."

"I am not," Mom replied indignantly. "I am not prejudiced, Joely, and even if I were, this isn't about Ricky."

"It's not?" Where was she going with this? I didn't know, but I folded my arms in defense.

"This is about you acting out. Your father and I both know you aren't happy about the baby, so now you're dating someone we don't approve of. Just to spite us. It's called the only-child syndrome, Joely."

"I—I—I . . ." I was so angry, I could only sputter. For one thing, it wasn't true! I really liked

100

Ricky. I *wasn't* going out with him just to annoy my parents, no matter what they thought! "I can't believe you said that!" I exploded finally, my voice filled with the hurt and bitterness I felt. "I'm not that shallow."

Right then my mom's eyes changed from confrontational to pleading, and she sighed heavily. "I didn't say you were shallow, honey, I just think you're out of your depth here. You're upset with us, and you're lashing out. That's not reasonable. So I won't allow it."

"Allow it?" My voice had fallen to a low, harsh whisper. "You can't tell me what to do," I added, feeling the blood drain from my face.

"Actually I can," Mom snapped, the edge back in her voice. "And I forbid you to go out with this boy alone, on a date."

Forbid? My hands were shaking with anger now, and I felt all my former excitement plummet to the floor. "Why are you doing this to me?" I muttered, feeling hot tears springing to my eyelids. "It's just a date," I said, sniffing miserably. "And there's *nothing wrong* with Ricky," I added hoarsely. "You just don't know him. But he's nice, and he doesn't deserve this!" That was when I broke down and really wept. All my hopes and thoughts about this special day, just a week away, shattered by one word from my mother: *forbid*.

Why did she have to put such a downer on things? I had started at cloud nine, but now I was getting closer to cloud four, or maybe I wasn't even

101

on the clouds anymore. My stomach had lost that floaty feeling, and it was replaced with a hard, tight knot. My face crumpled as I stared at Mom through my tears. Yup, the clouds were officially over. My mother had brought me down to earth. Hard.

But either Mom was still in hormonal swing or else my tears did the trick because she held up her hands while I was in the middle of a sobbing fit. "Okay, Joely, you win," she said quietly. "You want to go out with this boy, you go out with him. You're old enough to make your own judgment calls, and sooner or later you'll have to make decisions alone."

"Huh?" I sniffed, wiped my eyes with the kitchen towel, and blinked, confused, at my mom. "You're not forbidding me?"

"No. We won't stop you if you want to go on this date," Mom replied. "But I will encourage you to think seriously about *not* going."

"Well, I'm not listening to you," I croaked, my eyes glittering with tears. "I know him, and you don't."

For a moment Mom said nothing, just drummed her fingernails on the kitchen counter, like she does when she's thinking hard about a problem. "Honey," she said at last. "I know you think I'm against you, but it's your best interests I'm looking out for. You can go on this date if you want to, but I think you should watch out. Are you really ready to handle someone like Ricky? Have you thought about that?"

"You don't know anything about him, so I don't know why you're asking," I retorted huffily, rolling my eyes. This lecture was not only upsetting—it was getting boring!

"I know enough about Ricky," Mom countered. "Like the fact that he came to this house with a six-pack when your father and I weren't home. I saw him shoot out to his motorcycle when I came home. I decided not to say anything about it at the time, but . . ."

Oops! My eyes widened as I recalled the night Ricky had stopped over and brought beer. Did Mom *ever* miss anything?

"Ricky is a kid growing up too fast, Joely, and you're only fifteen. Drinking is bad enough. But what about sex? Didn't you yourself tell us that Ricky hangs out with an older crowd? What do you think that means?"

As my mom chattered on, I gulped and wished I'd never been so stupid as to try and make Ricky sound edgier than he even was, back when I was trying to get my parents' attention. Now it had all come back to bite me in the butt! And the truth was, although I hated to admit it, some of what my mom was saying was starting to unnerve me.

Ricky *was* more experienced than me—there were no two ways about that one. I wasn't a drinker, and I certainly had never had sex with anyone before. Not even close. But Ricky . . . ?

"I'll be fine," I assured my mom coldly at the end of her lecture. "I can handle myself."

My voice was firm and did the trick. Mom stopped talking, and I carried on cooking. But as I put the pasta into hot water, I couldn't help noticing the shake in my hands. *I can handle myself.* Could I really handle myself? No matter how much I didn't want her to be right, Mom had a point. Ricky was way more sophisticated than me. He hung out in bars, with cool, older people who smoked and drank and did stuff I'd only heard about.

And now that I'd accepted the date, would Ricky expect me to do things I wasn't going to be comfortable doing? Was the pressure officially on?

I didn't know. But I *had* said yes to a date.

Uh-oh.

Ricky

"Man, I think I'm gonna hurl," Andy Swensen panted as he staggered off the roller coaster. Then he grinned, held up the can of beer in his hand, and ran a hand through his hair. "Still didn't spill a drop," he added proudly. "Unlike you, Ramirez."

"Well, if you hurl, bro, then we're even," Jake said back, slurring slightly from his third beer. "Because I may have spilled the brew, but this here is Iron Stomach Ramirez!" Jake fake bowed and then lit a cigarette. "No one can hold their liquor better than me. Not even Lenci."

"*Especially* not Lenci," Andy chimed in as we

walked away from the ride. I shrugged and didn't answer. I didn't give a fig what anyone thought of my liquor-holding capacity. In fact, being at the town agricultural fair—which always used to be a fun excuse for drinking—somehow left me cold this year. Sure, I was there with my best buddies, but I don't know. Something about the traditions of drinking and then testing each other on the rides seemed kind of stupid this year.

Maybe I'd outgrown it?

I'd been coming to the fair for as long as I could remember. Everyone came. Even fancy folk like the Carmichaels. There's sheep showing, which was always kind of fun to crack up at, and then there's other dinky stuff like homemade-pie stalls and quilt sales. I'd give those a skip, but always, every year, I'd done the rides with my pals and put back a few beers while I was at it. Nobody checks you at the fair. It's run by old geezers who wouldn't know a twelve-year-old from a thirty-year-old, so you can do stuff like that.

But this year I couldn't get into it as much as I used to. Maybe it was just getting old because all things get old. Or maybe it was the fact that I was just days away from my date with Joely and still trying to figure out what I should do with her. Take her to a movie and then dinner? Just dinner? Where? My parents' restaurant? Or would that be too basic for her?

"Hey, bro, drink up, would you?" Andy squinted at me from underneath his gazillion freckles.

105

"You've been holding that beer, like, *all night,* man!"

I laughed and suddenly realized I'd been acting way too serious on a night when I should just be letting loose.

"Cheers," I said to Andy, and took a slug of the beer. I still didn't feel like getting drunk, but a few sips wouldn't hurt.

"Hi, Ricky!" A breathy voice floated over on the warm air, and I looked up to see Krista. She's a pal of Deena's. Goes to school in another county, so I don't know her well, but she's kind of a knockout, which means I've always noticed her. We all have.

"Hey, Krista. What's up?" I said, taking in her long, black hair and cool combat boots.

"Not much."

"Hi, Krista, what's going on?" Jake broke in, eager to get near Krista. He'd had a badass crush on her for years, so I stepped back and let him try to charm her, which was kind of funny since Jake was a little unsteady on his feet.

Deena and two other girls I didn't know joined us, and then we all started talking and hanging near the stupid games, where Jake and Andy tried to win stuffed bears for the girls by throwing hoops onto cones and shooting plastic goldfish in a barrel. Mostly I just smiled and sipped my beer. Warm, dusky night, pretty girls around us. I was starting to have fun.

"Hey, isn't that your girlfriend?" Jake spoke up as I was attempting to tell Krista about my job at the bike shop. "Buying *candy floss?*" he added mockingly, and I frowned at Jake to shut up as I looked across to a red-and-white-striped stand near the bumper cars.

Joely was there with her crowd, buying candy floss and caramel apples. She saw me just a second after I saw her, and we both smiled. She looked really pretty in a yellow summer dress, her hair in two braids. But although I wanted to go over and say hi, and I think she did too, I guess we both somehow picked up that now was not the time. So we just waved at each other, and I tried to hide the cigarette I was smoking. After all, I don't want her to think I'm full of bad habits. Even if I am.

"That's your girlfriend?" Krista inquired, her eyes flicking over to Joely, who by now was giggling with Shelby and her other gal pals.

"No, she's not my girlfriend," I said. "But she is a friend," I added quickly, feeling a flash of guilt for not sticking up for Joely in front of Krista, who was raising her eyebrows as if to say, "Why would you even know such a nerd?"

I smiled again at Joely, but the moment was a little weird for me. Somehow—although none of my friends actually said anything—it seemed a bit bizarre, even to me, that I was friends with Joely, who at that moment seemed like my total opposite. Eating candy floss. Giggling with Shelby and the rest of her tribe while I smoked cigarettes and got tipsy with mine.

And right then I wondered if there was even a point in trying to date a girl like Joely. Yes, she was beautiful and kind and smart. But that was also part of the problem. I'm not used to classy girls like her. I'm just not used to girls in yellow sundresses.

"She's hot for you," Andy cackled in my ear, holding his beer can up to Joely, who was pretending not to notice us but not doing a very good job.

Hot for you. I doubted that, but even if Joely did like me in that way—even if I managed to convince her I could be more than just a friend—that didn't change the fact that there was a real gulf between our worlds. Her friends would never dig me. And mine would definitely find her way too green.

And that's when something I'd never given much thought to hit me like a ton of bricks: Joely and I might end up liking each other enough to go out as a couple. . . . But who'd want to hang out with us?

Joely

"So what are you going to wear on this date with Ricky?" Catherine prodded as we waited on line for the roller coaster. "I think you should wear your red dress," she added with a devilish smile. "That will get his heart pounding!"

"Cath!" Shelby groaned with annoyance. "Haven't you heard *anything* Joely's been saying? She's *scared* of Ricky. Wearing red would only make things worse! It would be like a red flag to a *bull!*"

"*Shelby!*" I groaned. "That's *not* what I'm saying." I shook my head, but somehow I couldn't explain myself without getting my tongue twisted into knots. I'd spent the better part of an hour fretting about my date with Ricky. But how nervous was I? I wasn't sure. I didn't really think Ricky would hit me up for sex on a first date, and I didn't want my friends to think he was that type of guy either.

But still, I couldn't help the tremor of fear in my heart, and it had nothing to do with the roller coaster. One look at Ricky standing with all those downtown girls around him and the truth was pretty much a given: Ricky could have anyone he wanted. Which meant he must have had a lot of them.

Stop! I forced the thought from my mind. How did I know what Ricky did and who he did it with? And would I like it if someone presumed to know my story?

But I couldn't help it. I was scared. And my friends were only making it worse.

"Even if he doesn't try to go all the way with you, he'll definitely expect to do stuff," Shelby said somberly, and Catherine nodded in agreement.

Great! I gritted my teeth. I'd hoped my friends wouldn't reinforce my mother's fears about Ricky, but they'd actually been making me feel *more* terrified. And as we shuffled forward in line, I suddenly wished I wasn't going on the roller coaster. But like the date, there seemed no way to back out now.

"He's definitely a ladies' man," Catherine commented after they'd grilled me for the trillionth time about exactly where Ricky was taking me on our date (which, like I told them, I didn't know).

"Did you see how many of those townie girls were standing around him?" Melanie added. "Like moths to a flame!"

"Yeah," Shelby agreed. "He definitely gets around."

By this point I'd tried to shut my friends' voices out of my head, but I couldn't completely ignore what they'd said. Especially since I had just seen with my own eyes how the girls in Ricky's group reacted to him. Standing close, flirting, trying to get him to talk to them one-on-one. And now, instead of feeling flattered that such a popular tough guy had softened enough to ask me out on a date, I was absolutely, totally dreading it!

"Maybe I have lost my head. And let things get out of control," I said finally to my friends as they stopped their jabber for a moment. I sighed and explained that at first I liked hanging with Ricky. We'd just hit it off so well. "Plus it drove my parents crazy," I admitted, "and made them pay more attention to me, which was a bonus, although now I wish they'd *stop* paying so much attention to my affairs!"

"My parents would also flip out if I went out with Ricky," Catherine broke in, and we both rolled our eyes. Her parents were like mine: overprotective and a whole lot less liberal in practice than they thought they were!

"This is so *confusing*," I added with a frown.

"No, it's not."

I froze as I heard the familiar male voice behind me. Familiar, except for the coldness in it. *Ricky!* I turned and there he was, right behind us, his green eyes flashing.

"It's really simple," Ricky continued, clenching the muscles in his jaw. "Not as simple as your plan to use me to get back at your parents for having a baby—but there *is* a solution to your troubles."

I felt all the blood drain from me as I looked at the blank anger in Ricky's face. How long had he been standing there? Long enough, apparently, to get the wrong end of the stick because evidently he now thought I'd never even liked him!

"I can't believe I thought we were friends," Ricky said icily, his face a mask as I stood facing him in horror, my back to my friends.

"Ricky, wait," I interrupted him. "You heard wrong. Let me explain it. What I—"

But Ricky held up a hand and shook his head. He wasn't going to listen.

"Like I said, I have a solution for you, Joely," he snapped. "I'll make it easy on you. The date is off."

That's when I felt my heart drop like a stone to the pit of my stomach. "Rick—" My mouth was dry, and I could barely croak his name. But it didn't matter anyway. He was backing away, moving out of the line.

"Or maybe I'll keep the date," he added sarcastically as he inched away from me. "And just get one of the many girls I've slept with to fill in for you!"

He stared with piercing eyes then at Shelby, Catherine, Melanie, and me, and then without another word he turned and walked away.

And I just stood there. Wishing I could be anyone, anyone at all except me, Joely Carmichael: the girl with the biggest mouth, the girl with the worst instincts.

The biggest loser in the world.

Ricky

As I revved the engine into a screaming buzz, all I could think of was getting the hell out of there. Maybe riding as fast as I had been lately would help me calm down. Because I was definitely mad. Crazy angry, so angry, my heart felt like it was made of fire.

How could Joely have manipulated me like that just to get attention from her parents? I sped out onto the highway, picking up speed, still partly disbelieving even though I'd heard her telling her friends how she was only hanging with me because her parents hated me!

As if she doesn't have enough attention . . . spoiled . . . only-child princess . . . my thoughts were totally disjointed and furious, and I felt sickened to my gut.

Should have known better than to give a snob like Joely a chance . . .

She's not sweet—she's a scheming, heartless girl!

Suddenly everything that seemed fresh about

112

Joely now seemed like evidence against her. Even being a Mathlete counted against her, and my anger soared along with the moans from my engine. Being good at math just made Joely more of a natural for the kind of calculating, analytical thinking she'd needed to get what she wanted from me.

What a sap!

I'd been stupid, so stupid that all I wanted to do was just lose myself in the black night, lose myself in this road and the speed and the bright lights in front of me. . . . Except that the white lights are coming straight at me, and the skid of my brakes doesn't slow me down at all.

And I'm floating through the air and wondering where the lights came from . . . and the lights are really bright . . .

And now there's nothing but blackness.

Joely

Dear Ricky,

You'll never see this, so why am I writing it? Because maybe it'll help me get over the guilt I feel. I wish you could know how sorry I am, how much I wish I could turn back the clock on that night at the fair.

The thing is, Ricky, although I know

it looked that way to you, I never spent time with you just to spite my parents. I've always liked you. I've always wanted you to like me too. And then when we started hanging out, it made me really happy.

It's true that I was weak enough to let my parents think the worst of you when I could have stopped them from their prejudices. In that way I was really, really wrong and selfish. I wanted my parents to focus on me, so I used our friendship to my advantage.

But I swear to you, I never set out to be friends with you just to bug my parents. And I certainly never agreed to go out with you to upset them. I wanted that date more than anything.

Not that any of that matters anymore. Because I still screwed up. And no apology can change what happened. And I know I will pay for that for the rest of my life.

Joely

Seven

Joely

"COME IN, JOELY."

Mr. Lenci smiled weakly at me as I tentatively stepped into the Lenci home.

"You brought flowers. That's nice," Mr. Lenci added, gesturing at the bunch of red roses in my hand. Poor Mr. Lenci still looked in shock—his skin was gray, and he seemed older than when I'd seen him a few weeks ago.

Was it really just a few weeks ago?

It felt like a lifetime.

I cleared my throat nervously. What could I say? I didn't even know how to broach the subject of the accident. It had taken a lot just to get me to come here.

But Mr. Lenci didn't seem to need words, and he took me right into Ricky's room.

Slowly I lifted my eyes. Ricky lay in his bed,

propped up against a pile of pillows, a large white bandage down one side of his face and visible cuts running up and down his arms.

"A lucky guy," Mr. Lenci commented as he surveyed his son. "The way he rides that damn bike, he should have got a lot more than just a broken rib and a couple of cuts."

As Mr. Lenci left the room, I swallowed nervously. Guilt inflamed me, inside and out. I should have corrected Ricky's father. It was *my* fault that Ricky had had his accident. But I couldn't yet even find the words to say I was sorry to Ricky. I'd written a million letters I knew I'd never send, and now it all came down to this: his green eyes looking at me with so much distance in them. My hands shaking like leaves.

It was like we were total strangers.

But I had to speak. I had to tell him how sorry I was and at least try to explain that part of that whole awful night had been a misunderstanding.

"Ricky," I began softly. "I wanted to—"

But before I could even finish my sentence, Ricky turned his cheek so that he faced away from me and toward his bedroom window.

"Can we talk some other time?" Ricky said in a voice as cold and impersonal as a telephone operator's. "I'm tired."

Hot tears stung my eyes as I murmured my okays. And then, face burning, I turned, trembling, and fled the room. As I burst out of the Lenci home and down onto the driveway, the tears spilled

116

onto my cheeks without stopping. Seeing Ricky's cuts was bad. Seeing Ricky in pain was bad. But seeing him turn away from me was agonizing.

Ricky had turned his cheek because he couldn't bear to look at me.

And I just couldn't bear that.

Ricky

"He just spit up on me," I snapped at Carla as she lay filing her nails on the couch.

Carla raised an eyebrow. "He's a baby. What do you expect?"

I grunted and shifted Marco onto my lap. What did I expect? I expected that I could recuperate after a motorcycle accident without becoming a built-in baby-sitter! Okay, maybe that's an exaggeration, but after six days at home I was even starting to miss school! A real first.

"Okay, out with it. What are you in such a bad mood about?" Carla demanded as I shunted into an easy chair. I shrugged, didn't feel like answering, but I guess I was being kind of obvious, staring at Joely's flowers on the coffee table, like I'd been doing all morning.

"It's that rich girl, isn't it?" Carla probed.

Rich girl. That wasn't how I'd describe Joely but I didn't feel like sticking up for her right now, even though I did feel bad about everything. It was kind of low for me to allow her to feel guilty about the accident.

It wasn't her fault, but I hadn't said anything to her when she brought the flowers. I guess I wanted her to feel bad, even though an accident was bound to happen sooner or later, the way I'd been riding lately.

"It's her, right?" Carla repeated, and I frowned. Why couldn't she just get off my back? Let me have a private moment of misery?

"I just wiped out on my bike. Broke a rib. And you expect me to be sunny?" I shot back.

But Carla wasn't buying any of it, and sooner or later I just gave in and told her so she'd quit bugging me. Yeah. Joely was on my mind. I couldn't figure out if I'd been had or not. All I knew was that I was still really, really angry.

"You have a right to be," Carla said after I'd told her what had happened at the fair. "But Ricky, face facts. You're also to blame."

"For what?" I demanded as I handed a gurgling Marco back to Carla.

"For being a dreamer, that's what," Carla shot back impatiently. "Face it, buddy. Uptown girls and downtown boys don't mix. Except in Billy Joel songs," she added with a humorless smile.

Gloomily I looked back at Joely's flowers, regretting spilling my feelings to Carla. Of course she would only trash Joely. But I wasn't sure I could deal. Thing is, Carla's a straight talker, and she's been around the block. So she knows a thing or two. But I also wanted a fair perspective, which isn't something Carla could give me. Not after she got dumped by Pete.

118

"He was a rich kid. Like your Joely. He left me because of class issues or whatever his parents called it, and it sounds like your girl is just as impressionable. Letting her parents walk all over you like that." Carla sniffed and shook her head. "Forget her, Ricky. She can bring all the flowers she likes, but that's not going to change the situation."

Angrily I scratched at an itchy scab on my knee and then stared out the window. I hated to even think that what Carla was saying was true. But it sure made some sense. And now all I could do was wish I hadn't wasted my time. Yeah, I'd thought Joely was different from the other snobs at Edenvale, but apparently I was wrong. Things had gone sour between us, and who knew, maybe it was for the best. Better to cut things off before they start than have your heart broken later.

Or whatever.

"So . . . lucky you, you get to miss the last day of the school year," Carla said to make conversation with me after I'd sat for a long time in silence. "Next year you're a senior. And then it's over."

But the mention of school only made me feel worse. "I'm not going back," I said suddenly, surprising even myself with the words. I'd thought I'd figured all that out anyway. Decided to stay in school. But after they came out, the words felt right. I was glad I was missing the last day of school, and I would be glad if I never went back. I'd always hated it there, and maybe it was time to get real. Move on. Blow this town, once and for all.

"Sweetie, what's the matter?" Dad asked as he pushed open my bedroom door.

But I couldn't answer. I was too busy crying into my bedsheets.

"Joely . . ." Dad sat down gingerly on the bed next to me, ready to listen, but I couldn't talk about it.

All week I'd been walking around like a robot. Ever since Ricky had turned away from me, I couldn't stop thinking about it. I caused him to have an accident. It was my fault.

As a fresh round of tears welled up in my eyes, my dad looked at me with concern clouding his big, dark eyes. "What's wrong, honey?"

I gulped. A part of me wanted to burst out and tell him everything. But another part of me held back. I didn't want Dad to know I was jealous of the baby and had been scheming to get his and Mom's attention. That would only make me feel more rotten than I already did. Still, I needed to tell him something. Because I just felt too miserable carrying the guilt for Ricky's accident all by myself.

So I told Dad. Not everything. But the part about arguing with Ricky and how I'd caused the accident.

"He got upset with me because he overheard me talking about our date," I explained between rounds of Kleenex. "I told my friends some stuff about Ricky that bothered me, but he heard it out of context. And he left the fairground really upset

120

before I had a chance to explain. That's why he was riding so fast. That's why he didn't see the stop sign."

As sobs racked my body, my dad put his arms around me. Everything inside me felt jumbled up, but feeling my dad hugging me only made me want to cry more. I had been so selfish with Ricky. And maybe with my parents too. Some role model I would make as an older sister to the baby!

"But Joely," Dad began quietly after I'd finished telling my story. "You said yourself that your argument with Ricky was a misunderstanding. These things happen. You're not to blame."

"So why do I feel so awful?" I croaked. But I didn't expect Dad to answer. Nor did I expect him to understand why I needed to make things right with Ricky. After all, Dad hadn't wanted me to even be friends with him in the first place.

But then my father said something that really shocked me.

"Talk to him," Dad said firmly, looking me in the eye. "Tell him what's on your mind. Just because he didn't want to speak to you last week doesn't mean he'll never speak to you again."

Dad's words took me totally by surprise. I knew the last thing he wanted was for me to hang out with Ricky. Yet here he was, telling me to try and get through to him instead of being relieved that things weren't working out between us.

"It's important to do what you think is right, in your own heart," Dad continued, squeezing my hand. "So make him listen, however you can."

Hello? I blinked. "*You* think I should talk to him," I mumbled, still confused. This didn't sound like Dad! "You don't even *like* Ricky!" I finished.

"What I like or don't like isn't important right now," Dad said dismissively. "You know what's important, Joely. And for now, all you need from me is my support."

That's when the next round of tears pricked my eyelids, but I didn't cry. Instead I actually smiled, an activity so foreign, I'd almost forgotten how to do it. Dad and I were really connecting again! For the first time in what felt like forever.

"It's been a tough few months for you," Dad said. "Lots of new adjustments."

"I guess." I sighed, picturing the upheavals and responsibilities that lay just around the corner. But then I smiled again as Dad's eyes fell on the photo on my nightstand. Me and Dad when I was about two years old. On the shores of Lake Superior.

"I remember this." Dad smiled fondly as he picked up the framed picture. "My little girl," he added affectionately, tussling my hair.

"And now you're getting a new baby," I blurted, and then instantly regretted how that sounded: jealous.

But Dad didn't frown or tell me I was being childish, which I knew I was being. Instead he just hugged me again. "You'll always be my first little girl. No one can change that."

A warmth spread through my heart as Dad blew

me a kiss before leaving my room. It had been a long time since I'd felt close with my dad like that, but I knew what he'd said would always stay with me. No matter how much the new baby would change things, I would always be Dad's first little girl. And there was something kind of special about that.

But although my father had helped me put a bit more of a positive spin on my evening's crying session, I fell asleep with a splinter of sadness in my heart. The moment when Ricky asked me out on a date seemed a million years ago.

And nothing I could do would ever bring it back.

Eight

Joely

"OUR LAST DAY of being juniors!" Shelby proclaimed excitedly as she emptied her locker, her eyes sparkling alongside her grin. "Next time we walk these hallways, we'll be seniors!"

"Yeah," I said absently, scanning the hallway. I had bigger things on my mind than grade changes. I was looking for Ricky. Hoping he'd made it to school for the last day.

But as I caught sight of Deena and Jake and a few others from Ricky's crowd, my face fell. If Ricky were back at school, he'd be with them.

Or maybe not, I told myself hopefully, striding toward Ricky's friends. Ricky could be a lot of places. Maybe he was trying to convince Mr. Bailey to give him a passing math grade. Or maybe he was still on his way to school . . . and taking longer because he had to get a ride in with his dad. *Yeah, that makes sense,* I thought, picturing Ricky's mangled bike, which had been totaled in the accident.

But whatever the story, I had to find Ricky. And I lifted my chin to make myself feel extra confident. I had psyched myself up for this day, big time. After my dad's empowering lecture, I'd thought I would give Ricky a call and explain myself.

But then I'd gotten cold feet. And after a weekend of nerve jangling, I'd finally realized that Ricky and I had to talk face-to-face. Today.

"Hey, Jake," I said, trying to keep my voice casual as I approached Ricky's best friend. "Ricky around?"

"No." Jake's voice was flat and cold, but I tried not to make anything of it. Jake might hate me, but like Ricky, he didn't know the full story.

"Is he coming in today?" I persisted as Deena shot me a sneery look, which I tried to ignore. "To get his stuff?" I added.

"Ricky's not coming back to school," Jake replied, leaning against the wall and fixing me with a look of pure contempt. "Ever."

I froze, rooted to the spot. *Ever?*

"B-but why not?" I stammered, my composure faltering.

"He hates it," Deena replied, and she didn't have to add the words "and you too" for me to understand the implications of her ice-toned voice.

And with that, both Deena and Jake turned to each other and carried on chatting as if I wasn't even there. As if they hadn't just dropped a bomb at my feet.

Ricky wasn't coming back to school. Why?

But although my knees felt suddenly wobbly, and I felt the full force of Ricky's friends' hatred and my own shocked surprise and confusion that he had dropped out of school, I forced myself to calm down and be strong and focus on what I set out to do. Words from my dad's pep talk came back to me. *Do what you think is right, in your own heart.*

In my heart I knew I hadn't used Ricky. And I knew I needed to tell him that. For now, that was all that mattered.

Ricky

"Coming!" I shouted as the doorbell rang for the second time, and I managed to get Marco to hold still while I finished changing him and put him down for his nap. He'd been fussy all morning, ever since Carla had left for her first community-college class. I guess both me and Marco were in a bad mood.

"Joely?"

I blinked as I looked at her, standing there on the front steps in the sunlight. *What's she doing here?* I'd thought I made myself clear enough when she last came. I'd been rude to her then. So why had she come back for more?

"Can I come in?" she asked uncertainly. I shrugged and made way for her. *This is going to be awkward,* I thought as I headed to the kitchen to fetch us some lemonade. It was boiling hot in the house. And we were uncomfortable enough already, just being in the same room!

"Do you want to sit out in the yard?" I asked Joely, handing her the lemonade.

"Sure," she said nervously.

Silently we arranged ourselves out on the steps. You could cut the air between us with a knife—and I'm not talking about the stifling heat of an early summer.

After a few minutes of this, I was about to call a time-out and send the girl on her way. What was the point of all that weirdness if we could just go back to ignoring each other? I was all for it, but I was also curious as to why she was showing her face again. An apology wouldn't do much. . . . Still, I guess I thought it was better than nothing.

But Joely just sat there squirming, and now I was ready to drop the whole thing.

"Look," I began, kind of harshly. "I think you should—"

But before I could finish, she broke in. "Ricky, I'm sorry," she said in a voice so miserable, it stopped me in my tracks. "I am so sorry I caused your accident. I—" Her voice wobbled, and she looked at her feet.

But now it was my turn to feel rotten. Joely hadn't caused my accident. I was the one on the motorcycle, and I couldn't rightly blame her for it. Yet I said nothing. I guess I just didn't feel like being fair right now. Not after being used.

"If you'd just let me tell you what really happened," Joely ventured as I set down my lemonade and folded my arms. "Because it's not like you think."

"Oh yeah?" My voice was brittle, but although I felt like getting up and walking away, somehow I just didn't. There was something in her voice that stopped me. Some kind of softness. It kept me on the steps, but I wasn't expecting much.

"I know you think I engineered everything between us just to spite my parents," Joely began. "But I didn't. It's true they don't approve of you," she continued in a low voice. "But that's not why I accepted the date."

I'd been staring stone-faced out toward my mom's roses, but now I turned to look at Joely full on. "Then why did you?"

Joely hesitated, and I realized her hands were shaking. But she looked me in the eye anyway. "Because I like you," she replied quietly.

"You like me," I repeated dubiously. Her voice was sincere, but Joely, like me? She had a funny way of showing it! After all, I'd heard her telling her friends how freaked out she was about our date! I'd heard with my own ears also how she'd gotten off on the fact that her parents were worried I was too fast for her . . . or whatever the hell they thought.

"Doesn't a girl who likes a guy stick up for him when her stuck-up parents trip out over his hairstyle?" I shot back, and then took an extra-big gulp of my lemonade to cool the angry, hot feeling in the pit of my stomach. Just thinking of Joely's parents made me mad. They didn't know me. But they thought they had me all figured out.

"It's not your hairstyle," Joely replied softly. "It's the fact that I'm . . . well . . . kind of not a big dater," she mumbled. "So my parents are real protective. And conservative," she added. "I'm not defending them. They're scared of guys with motorcycles."

Fair point, I thought grudgingly. I mean, I had after all just wiped out, big time! I couldn't blame the Carmichaels for being edgy on that front. But I wasn't buying Joely's other defense of her parental unit.

"Not a big dater? You date, Joely. Come on." I had no patience for this. Joely was a popular girl in her preppy world. I was sure she'd gone out with a handful of the Tommy Hilfiger types in our class.

"I've been on two dates in my whole life."

For a moment I forgot my anger. I was kind of surprised. Two dates? Sure, I knew Joely was an innocent type, but I wasn't blind either. Someone as pretty as Joely didn't have only two dates to her name. Or did she?

"I mean, I've gone out in groups, of course," Joely added hastily, picking at some flaking nail polish on her thumbnail, her cheeks turning pink. "But that's the truth: two dates. One last year and one this year. Both so boring, I almost fell asleep," she joked weakly.

I said nothing, but mentally I was checking

through my own dating history. And that's when I realized I wasn't big Dater Man myself. Yeah, I'd had a thing going on with a girl here and there. But dates? Like, formally asking someone to dinner and/or movies? Hardly any. "I'm not a serial dater either," I said. "I hang out with my group and stuff, but I'm no Valentino. Or Casanova. Even though I'm Italian," I quipped.

"Hardly any dates? You? Are you kidding me?" Joely squeaked, forgetting her awkwardness for a moment.

"Nope." I shook my head, wondering whether I should be insulted or amused that Joely thought I was such a player.

Meanwhile she smiled at me. I was glad to see that she looked more relaxed. "Well, I guess we have two things in common now," she said. "New babies in the family and a lack in the dating-history department."

"I guess," I replied, and we both laughed. "Plus we both like Frank Sinatra," I reminded Joely.

"And we go to the same school . . . right?" Her expression changed from a grin to a brow-furrowing concern. *So she's heard. . . .*

"Not anymore," I said quietly, taking a Marlboro from the box in my pocket. "I'm not going back to school. I'm moving to Chicago to work in my uncle's garage. I'll do my GED part-time," I added, and then lit up my smoke. "Leaving in a couple of weeks."

The last sentence just came out of my mouth. I

hadn't actually decided on when I was leaving yet. Hadn't even told my folks. But saying it made me realize that in the back of my mind, I had made my plans. It was time to go.

"Oh." Joely's voice was very small, and a look of disappointment washed over her face. A look I didn't need. But how could I explain to her that I just didn't belong in school? How do you explain that stuff to someone who gets all A's and is headed off to some fancy college her parents have been planning for all of her life?

The truth is, you can't. Because they'll just try to change your mind. People like Joely don't understand why others drop out of school. I took a drag of my cigarette, tension creeping back into me. And right then, looking at Joely's pale, sad-looking face, I realized it was time for her to go. We'd had an okay conversation, as far as conversations go, but I could see she didn't know what to say next. Nor did I.

Talking—the one thing that had always been easy for us—was no longer easy.

"I'll walk you to the door," I said abruptly, standing up. Immediately I felt bad about my tone. I didn't hate Joely; I just didn't think we had anything left to say, and I definitely wasn't into hearing any judgments about my quitting school. But that didn't mean I should have been rude. "By the way," I added, putting a hand on her shoulder as she stood at the front door, "the accident wasn't your fault."

"Yes, it was." Joely's cheeks were pink, and her

shoulder was warm. In that moment it felt like we could be honest again without upsetting each other. Say anything that came to mind. Be friends.

But the moment was fast fading. I was headed out of town. And Joely had her own plans.

I let go of Joely's shoulder. "I would have had an accident anyway," I told her. "I ride too fast."

"Well . . ." Joely took a deep breath and then looked at me as if waiting for me to say something else. But I was all done. "Maybe we'll see each other in Chicago," Joely suggested timidly. "I'll be there for Mathlympics in July, remember?"

"Yeah, maybe." *Maybe, but doubtful,* I thought. Chicago's a big town. We'd probably miss each other completely.

"I'd better go," Joely said, and I nodded.

"Take it easy," I said.

And then I shut the door, a little too fast. But it was for the best.

Ever since Ricky told me that he's leaving, I can't stop thinking in "what-ifs." What if we'd gone on a date? Would that have changed anything, or am I just fooling myself? What if I'd never gone to the town fair? What if I'd decided not to go on the roller coaster after all?

That game can drive you crazy. I don't know the answers to my what-ifs, and I never will. The only thing I do know is that I feel miserable that Ricky's leaving town. And I wish I could tell him that, but it's been three days since I saw him, and I got the distinct feeling then that he didn't want to stay friends.

Three days, no phone calls, nothing. We're back to our separate worlds.

And as if my life isn't bad enough, my mom is now so heavily pregnant that I have to do absolutely everything. Only four and a half weeks to go until the baby comes.

I can't remember when I've ever felt this low. My life feels like a bad joke with no punch line. I'm not even looking forward to going to Chicago for the Mathlympics on July 7. Even though that will be my last week of prebaby freedom.

But it's like I just don't care anymore.

I really, really, really wish I could see Ricky again. But what can I do? I've done my best to make him realize that I want to be his friend.

But he's made it clear: he's moving out and moving on.

End of story.

Ricky

"It won't be hard for you to replace me," I said to Spike as we sat outside Spike's Bike with sodas.

Spike grunted and shook his head as if he still couldn't believe what I'd told him. But he would have to believe it. Because my decision was final. I was splitting. For good.

"Kid, this is not smart," Spike told me, still shaking his head. "I'm not just saying this because you're leaving me. Heck, I knew this wouldn't last forever. You're too young to hang out with old Spike forever." He cracked a thin smile beneath his mustache. "But quitting school? I thought you'd worked through that one. What changed?"

I shrugged. I didn't feel like a lecture from Spike. Truth is, I didn't feel like examining my decision up close anyway. I had decided to quit on a gut instinct that it was what I needed to do. But I knew if I started to pick apart my reasons, they would flake away like cheap paint on a beat-up bike.

"I just need to bail," I said to Spike honestly. "I want to go."

"Why?" Spike persisted, and I groaned and ran a grease-speckled hand through my hair.

"I dunno. Maybe because my house is crazy. Maybe because I just had an accident and I feel I need something good in my life. Some change. New people." I thought of Joely then and pushed the image of her out of my head. I couldn't think about her too much because it was too confusing. A part of me was relieved to be ditching the friendship. We were running on different tracks, and stuff had soured between us.

But another part of me felt like I'd be sorry someday. Joely's a unique girl. And there would be other girls—plenty of them to choose from in Chicago—but I doubted I'd ever meet one like her. I just didn't run in those circles.

"Look, Rick, I hate to act like Mr. Been There, Done That, but I'm telling you from experience, think again," Spike said, fixing me with his piercing eyes. "So you've hit a few speed bumps in the road. Doesn't mean you have to abandon your course altogether."

I sighed. Spike's words bugged me, but they also struck a chord. I knew I was running away, and it felt weak, but I didn't want to stay in Edenvale either.

". . . Just through the end of senior year, kid," Spike advised. "Then you'll be ready. Chicago's not going anywhere, you know."

I said nothing, but Spike's words were getting through even though I wished to God they didn't make any sense.

Problem was, I knew my hitting the road wasn't

a good decision. My folks would be really freaked, and they'd had a lot to deal with lately. Carla would also be upset. I'd been a big help to her. Cutting out would be bad for her. And for Marco.

But sooner or later you've got to get a life. Your own life, my inner voice told me. And that's when I knew I had to stick to my guns. Yeah, my decision didn't make a whole lot of sense. But then neither did anyone's risk-taking moment. That's what it was all about. Running with an idea. Not letting anyone tell you different.

"I have to go," I said to Spike, then picked up the washcloth next to me and started greasing up the next bike on the production line. Spike sighed, but I ignored him and focused on the job. And on staying positive. I was headed for Chicago. And I wasn't going to have any regrets.

Except maybe Joely. I would have liked to take her out on that date. Okay, so we might not be made for each other, but we'd been good friends . . . most of the time.

Too bad it all got so screwed up.

Maybe I would call her up in Chicago. We could grab some coffee or something.

Or maybe that would be too weird. With Shelby stuck to her side like a limpet.

Nah.

I worked slowly and tried to figure out what I should do. I guess I had a nagging bad feeling about the way I'd said good-bye to Joely almost a week ago. Not exactly a real good-bye.

I should call her, I thought suddenly. *Let her know I really don't have any hard feelings.* I could do that.

But almost instantly I chickened out. Chances were, she'd had enough of me.

I took a slug of my Pepsi, tightened my jaw, and went back to work. It seemed like the one thing I could figure out without thinking. Everything else—Joely, Chicago, leaving Marco, leaving school—just seemed like a major head case.

But no matter how hard I worked, I couldn't lose the worry that I was making not one mistake. But many mistakes.

And that's when I decided I wouldn't think about anything anymore. I would just go on pure instinct. From now on.

Like moving to Chicago.

Like putting down my tools and standing up.

Like finding a quarter and telling Spike I'd be right back.

"There's something I have to do," I told him. And then I walked to the pay phone before I had a chance to think twice.

Nine

Joely

I HOPE I don't look too dressy . . . or too casual!
My heart bumped painfully against my
chest as I made my way down the staircase, wondering if after all the outfit changes, I'd made the
right choice: pale pink tube top and a denim skirt.
Red Candies. *Or maybe I should have gone for
Skechers?* It was too hard to figure out, and I swallowed nervously, tasting the Luvstruck pink lipstick
I had hesitated over for so long because it was either
too subtle or too raunchy and I was somehow unable to decide which. *Chill out!* I commanded myself as I walked into the kitchen. I had to calm
down. But my hands felt light and fluttery. Almost
as light and fluttery as my stomach. Because Ricky
would be arriving any moment now.

I smiled to myself as I poured myself a glass of
cold water from the pitcher on the kitchen counter.

Ricky's phone call had come completely out of the blue. One minute I was moping in my room, the next he was asking me out to dinner!

And so the past two days had been one big stomach-knotting but exhilarating anticipation of the date. Mixed in with a kind of happy confusion. Why Ricky had changed his mind and decided to hang with me again I did not know. But I wasn't complaining.

"Can I get you anything?" I asked Mom brightly, walking into the sitting room to where she lay on the couch. Mom was three weeks away from delivery, and she looked it.

"Just some water with lemon, please." Mom sighed, and I quickly got a tall glass and poured. Poor Mom, she really did look uncomfortable. It was late June, too hot to be pregnant. Her ankles were swollen, and she seemed really tired now all of the time.

But not too tired to raise an eyebrow at my makeup, apparently.

"That's a lot of lipstick, honey," Mom said pointedly, fixing me with a classic mom look (i.e., a look that was both critical and yet subtle at the same time . . . so that you, object of the criticism, couldn't accuse her of looking at you critically without sounding hypersensitive!).

"No, it's not," I shot back swiftly. But a few moments later I mashed my lips together and found they really were gummy with color! So I dabbed some away, anxious not to overdo it.

"Better?" I asked Mom, a little sullenly, and she nodded with a faint smile.

I knew Mom still didn't approve of my dating Ricky, but as she lay on the couch, I silently willed her to be nice to him for my sake. Because no matter what, I was going on this date. And if my mother did anything to make Ricky uncomfortable, I'd—

Dingdong.

He was here!

My heart somersaulted against my ribs, and I took a deep breath for composure before going to the door. *Please God,* I prayed silently. *Please may Mom be nice to Ricky. And please may Ricky not arrive on his motorcycle!* He knew better than that . . . didn't he?

"Hi, Joely."

I tried not to ogle, but Ricky looked so drop-dead handsome. He was all spruced up—his hair still spiked but wetted down so that it looked fifties-ish. He wore a crisp, white, collared shirt, and his pants were pressed too! *Wow!* I grinned, impressed that Ricky would go to all this trouble for me. He really did look great, without losing his coolness. Over his fancy shirt, for example, he wore his biker jacket. And although his boots were polished, they were still biker boots.

In other words, he was still Ricky.

"Hello, Mrs. Carmichael," Ricky said stiffly as I led him into the sitting room.

"Hello, Ricky."

Mom sounded pleasant enough, but I could see

her looking Ricky up and down as if she had x-ray vision and could see something the rest of us mortals couldn't.

As for Ricky, he was shifting uncomfortably from one foot to the other, obviously highly aware of my mom's unspoken disapproval.

My face darkened, and I shot Mom a warning look. Gone was my sympathy for my pregnant, tired-out mom, alone at home on a hot night. She'd promised she would stay out of my business and let me run my own life. Yet she was staring at Ricky like he'd just brought bubonic plague into the house!

Be nice or you'll regret it! I willed Mom, cranking my stare up to a full-on glare.

"Where are you going tonight?" Mom's voice shifted to a lighter note, and I relaxed my jaw. Evidently she'd picked up on my look and was making an effort to be nicer.

But suddenly Ricky seemed even more self-conscious, and he jammed his hands into his pockets. "We're, uh, going to the, I mean—" he stammered. I cringed! I'd never seen Ricky nervous. It was weird. Weirdly heartbreaking! But I couldn't even help him out because *I* didn't know where he was taking me on our date. "My, uh, parents have a restaurant," he finished finally. "Lenci's on Main. We'll start our evening there."

And that's when my mom grimaced, as if Ricky had just suggested a chicken-wings special at a local biker dive. "Mom!" I snapped, unable to control

142

myself as her face contorted again. "What's the prob—"

"Mrs. Carmichael?" Ricky interrupted me. "Are you okay?"

"I'm . . . I—" Mom gasped. And right then I knew it wasn't her daughter's dinner date that had her so stressed. It was something else.

"I think I'm in labor!" Mom's face was stricken with shock, and then another tremor of pain overcame her and she doubled over.

"Mom?" Instantly my anger disappeared and I was left with a terrible, numb dread. Labor? She was three weeks away from her due date!

"Joely, get your dad on the phone," Ricky commanded swiftly. "Do it!" he added as I stared at him, still in shock, unable to move.

And that's when everything got blurry. Everything except the sound of Ricky's voice. Unlike earlier, he sounded totally confident and in control now as he encouraged my mom to take deep breaths.

"Dr. Carmichael's on rotation, but I'll try to page him," Dad's secretary said as I gripped the phone.

"Okay, we're running out of time," Ricky declared as Mom groaned through another burst of contractions. "I'm taking her to the car," he added, helping Mom to her feet.

As Ricky helped Mom up, all I could do was stand there like a block of wood. My head was spinning. What if we didn't get to the hospital in time?

But Ricky was in total-calm mode, even though he was moving like lightning. Once he'd gotten Mom into the backseat of Carla's Chevy and wrapped up in a blanket, he leaped into the front seat and screeched us out of the driveway in two seconds flat. "Deep breath in, Mrs. Carmichael . . . hold . . . and out," Ricky soothed, breathing in time with my mother, whose face was a mask of white panic. But something about Ricky's voice seemed to be doing the trick because by the time we hit the highway, Mom was doing her Lamaze like a pro.

"You know this stuff?" I murmured to Ricky, gripping the dashboard as we careened toward the hospital.

"I can fake it," Ricky replied in a low voice. "Went to Carla's Lamaze class. All of one time," he whispered with a grim smile. "But don't panic!"

Mom's cell phone, which I had in my hand, bleeped finally just as we neared the hospital gates. Dad. At last!

"We're ready for her—don't worry, sweetheart, she'll be fine," Dad said, his voice steady.

But neither Dad nor Ricky could calm me. I felt like I had no blood in my veins. Like I might faint. I knew I had to be strong for Mom . . . but I didn't think I was going to make it.

"Dennis?" Mom panted, grabbing the phone from me. "I don't think I can wait!" she shouted before another giant wave of pain hit her and she shrieked, sending shivers down my spine.

"Hold on, Mrs. Carmichael. Almost there!"

Ricky yelled, flooring the accelerator. And that's when I shut my eyes, unable to cope with whatever was next: would Mom have a baby *after* we crashed or before? *Oh God!*

And then suddenly we were there! Paramedics rushed to get Mom up to delivery, and all I could see was a flash of white coats. And Ricky, standing next to me, his hands shaking like leaves.

Amazed, I just stared at him. Only now did it actually hit me how terrified he'd been. But he'd put on a brave show. For Mom's sake. For mine. "Thank you," I whispered in a trembling voice, relief making me weak in the knees as I saw the doctors wheel Mom into the maternity ward. Whatever happened to my mother now, at least she was in the hospital, safely in the hands of professionals.

"Joely?" I turned to see my dad. "She'll be okay," Dad soothed as my eyes glinted with tears. Suddenly I just felt overwhelmed. "And what about the baby?" I asked nervously. "It's too soon."

"Don't worry," Dad said, squeezing me into a hug before turning to Ricky. "As for you, young man . . ."

Ricky swallowed nervously, and I looked up from the folds of Dad's lab coat. *Huh?* Was Dad mad at Ricky? Why? For driving too fast?

". . . you are one quick-thinking guy," Dad finished with a smile. His eyes shone in admiration, and he shook his head in amazement. "You got my wife over here in one piece. I'm truly grateful, Ricky."

"That's okay." Ricky shrugged, but I could see he was pleased, and as Dad stretched out his hand and gripped Ricky's into a handshake, I felt a little burst of warmth rippling through my insides. Dad liked Ricky. Admired him, even!

After the night from hell, this was a nice moment.

"I should get going," Ricky said softly, and I sighed.

"I'll walk you out."

As we walked back to the car, I felt so many things: terror about what lay ahead, like whether or not the baby would be okay. And relief that we'd made it to the hospital. All these big emotions swept through me, but there was also a place for one more: regret.

It was a small thing under the circumstances, but I felt sad that the date had been ruined!

"I guess the baby couldn't wait," I said with a rueful smile as we arrived at the Chevy.

"Yeah, too bad," Ricky said. "I'm sorry our date didn't happen," he added. "But I guess other things just keep getting in the way. Maybe that's just how it is between us."

"I guess." I bit my lip. I knew what he meant. It was a little strange that both times we'd planned on a date, it hadn't panned out. It was starting to seem like more than just coincidence. Like fate or something.

But fate could be changed too!

"Maybe we could go out for coffee . . . ?" I suggested hopefully. I knew Ricky was leaving in just a few days, but it was still possible for us to try this date thing . . . right?

But Ricky didn't answer. Instead he leaned over and pecked me on the cheek. His lips were dry as they brushed my skin, and I felt a little tingle of excitement in the pit of my stomach. But then without a word Ricky got into his car and drove away, before I had a chance to get an answer from him. Before I had a chance to kiss him back.

I stood and waved for a few moments before heading back inside. I waved until I couldn't see Ricky anymore, and I tried to ignore the feeling I had.

The feeling that somehow I wouldn't be seeing Ricky Lenci again.

Ricky

"I've got something to tell you," I said to Ma as she placed a plate of chicken parmigiano in front of me. We were in the kitchen of the restaurant, and despite the smell of Pop's chicken parmigiano, I felt suddenly not hungry at all.

Maybe it was the strain of the evening—getting Joely's mom to the hospital had been pretty nerve-racking. Or maybe it was the fact that what I was about to say would send my folks into a freak-out. For sure.

"What is it?" Ma probed as Pop frowned and wiped flour off his hands.

I swallowed. How would I break the news?

Maybe the best way would just be to blurt it out.

"I'm quitting school. I'm leaving for Chicago to work in Uncle Tony's garage."

"You *what?*" Mom shrieked, while Pop stood there in stunned silence.

"You heard me, Ma."

"No." Ma shook her head briskly, her curls springing back and forth, her eyes flashing angrily. "You are *not* quitting school. It's not an option, is it, Ricardo?" she added, glaring at Pop for backup.

But I wasn't listening. Ma started ranting, rattling a million and one reasons why I could not leave home, but I just sat there, waiting for her to finish. She was wasting her breath. My mind was made up.

"I won't let you," Ma finished, still shaking her head vigorously.

"I'm sorry, Ma, but it's decided," I replied quietly. But she refused to give up and started a fresh round of shouting.

"I'm too old to be ordered around!" I shot back after Ma's third burst of fire. "I'm sorry you don't like it, but it's too bad. This is my decision! You can't tell me what to do with my life!"

And that's when Ma started weeping. Which really tugged on my heartstrings. Ma always knew how to make me feel guilty, and as I sat there watching Pop try to comfort her, I felt lower down on the food chain than a one-celled amoeba.

Don't let this get to you, I coached myself as Ma

stared angrily at me with tear-filled eyes. I had to be strong. Even though I felt bad about leaving Pop and Ma, for leaving Marco and Carla, I had to leave this town. It had stifled me for too long. And I had a right to break free.

No matter how much it hurt.

"Look, Ma," I began, taking her hand in both of mine. "I'm not leaving you. I'm just leaving town. I'll be okay. And I'll make something of myself, I promise."

"At least stay in school!" Ma pleaded as I gave her hand another squeeze. "Please, Ricky, get your education."

"I'll think it over," I promised. But I didn't really mean it. It was time for me to hit the road and start a different kind of life. And although I felt sad sitting there in Pop's kitchen, knowing that I was going to be leaving my family behind, I knew I had to get out on the open road and see where it took me.

You only regret what you don't do, right?

That thought brought Joely to mind. I guess I would always regret that we'd never had a chance to spend an evening together, out on a date. But Joely and me, we obviously weren't meant to be. Way too many speed bumps there.

Joely

"Mom is going to be just fine," Dad said soothingly, putting his arm around my shoulders as I sat numbly outside the delivery room. "They're prepping her for a cesarean."

"I want to go in," I said tearfully, but Dad shook his head. It was a doctors-only situation. Or maybe Dad was just saying that? Maybe Mom and the baby were really in trouble and he didn't want me to know it?

This last thought was too much, and I just broke down into sobs.

All I could think of was how terrible I'd been to Mom and how awful I'd been about the baby. What if something happened? What if it was my fault? After all, for so long I'd wished my parents weren't having a baby. Maybe now my wish was going to come true.

It was the worst, most painful moment of my life.

"Honey, really, Mom is going to be just fine. And the baby," Dad promised, handing me a Kleenex. "The baby is only a few weeks premature. It happens all the time."

"Are you sure?" I sniffed.

"I'm a doctor, aren't I?" Dad replied with a smile.

"You're a neurologist," I shot back with a tearful smile. But I did feel better. Dad didn't look that worried, and as he headed back in for the delivery, he blew me a kiss.

I took a deep, deep breath then and sank onto a hard hospital couch. What a night! The old Joely would have been mad that the baby had ruined my date . . . but now all I could do was pray that the baby would be healthy.

"Joely?"

I looked up, startled to see my dad back so soon. But there he was. Grinning.

"Come inside. We want to introduce you to someone."

I stood up on shaking legs. My head felt like a helium balloon, and my heart was beating away like a Duracell bunny gone out of control. Slowly, as if I were in some kind of dream, I put one foot in front of the other and walked into the delivery room. And there they were.

Mom looked up at me with tearful, shining eyes. In her arms was a tiny, pink, mewling little bundle.

"Joely, meet your sister, Mary," Mom said, holding out a hand to me.

Your sister. Mary. They'd chosen the name I liked!

With still trembling legs I neared the bed and looked down into the smallest, scrunchiest pink face I'd ever seen. Mary. My sister. I was a sister to someone. It was the weirdest feeling in the world. But it was also kind of neat.

As I looked at Mary, at her tiny little fingers and closed eyelids fringed with long black lashes, it really hit me: I was going to be responsible for someone this tiny! I would have to help her learn to walk and learn to talk. I'd have to give her advice on clothes, makeup, dating. . . . Whoa! I blinked.

Getting ahead of yourself there! But looking at Mary, I found it hard not to imagine all the things I would have to be. I was a sister now.

"Isn't she beautiful?" Mom whispered, and I nodded. Mom and I both smiled at each other then. And all the tension between us, all the hard edges in our attitudes toward each other these past months, melted away. I was just glad that Mom was fine. And glad that Mary was too.

"Time to take her now," a nurse said, and I looked confused as Mary got whisked away.

"She will need to be in an incubator," Dad explained. "But just for a few days. She's going to be fine," he reassured me as a look of alarm crept onto my face.

I swallowed. Suddenly I felt the need to sit down. All these weird emotions were churning inside me. I was totally surprised by the wave of concern that engulfed me when the nurse removed Mary. Were all older sisters like that? Protective?

I felt so strange. My feelings for Mary were so unexpected. And something had changed between me and Mom too. Sure, I still thought it was crazy that my parents were having a baby so late in life, but it wasn't Mary's fault. It wasn't anyone's fault. It was just life.

"You have to thank Ricky for me," Mom said as Dad and I stood up to go so she could rest. "He did a remarkable thing," she added, with a tired but warm smile. "Invite him to dinner some night, would you, Joely?"

"Okay," I mumbled, and tried to smile back. But the thought of Ricky just made me feel sad. He would be gone soon, and there was nothing I could do about that. It was so ironic: I finally had my mom's blessing. But it was probably too little, too late.

Ten

Ricky

"MA, I DON'T need another lecture!" I growled as I threw clothes into my duffel bag. "Jeez!"

But the woman hadn't given up since the moment I'd told her I was splitting. Even now, I was planning to bail tomorrow and she still thought she could change my mind.

"I'm outta here. It's done," I muttered. But the decisiveness in my voice was a little faked.

The truth of it is, although I do my best to tune out Ma, the woman has a very logical brain on her. And the more she babbled away about why I ought to stay in Edenvale, the more shaky I was feeling about going. A part of me wasn't ready to leave Edenvale. Yet. Not that I'd let on, but the guilt was starting to get me down. Guilt and maybe even a

155

fear that I was running *away* from Edenvale instead of running *to* Chicago. There's a difference between the two ideas, and I was starting to feel it. One was a weak decision. No points for guessing which.

Which was why I wanted to finish packing. Maybe I would leave early. Before anyone could change my mind.

But although I'd managed to successfully drive Ma out of my bedroom, I suddenly couldn't finish getting my stuff together. Alone, I felt even more unsure. What was I doing? Why was I quitting school when I had only one lousy year left? Yeah, this town was a small-minded dump, but a big city like Chicago . . . ? Who was I kidding? It could swallow me whole.

Annoyed at myself, I left my room and made for the backyard. Outside, looking at Ma's roses, I felt a little calmer, and I lit a smoke and stared up at the sky in silence. It was a hot day. Superhot. The kind of day when thinking hurt.

But I couldn't turn off my brain. Warring voices, arguments for Chicago, arguments against.

I kicked a loose piece of gravel and wished I could just switch off my mind. But the longer I stayed outside, the more I realized I was being an idiot. Chicago wasn't going anywhere, like Spike said. So why did I have to figure it out now? It was so obvious I had reservations. And I was the one who would get screwed if I made the wrong choice. Me and me alone.

I stubbed out the cigarette. *Stay,* my inner voice told me. *For a while.*

Then it was like I could suddenly breathe. The pressure was off. I would stay until I felt totally ready to go. Whenever that was.

Right then I felt a kind of excited, happy feeling. Maybe I'd just kick back and enjoy the summer. Maybe I'd even get to go out on that date with Joely after all.

But then I thought again. Maybe it would be better to just let Joely get on with her summer. Yeah, her parents were grateful to me for getting Mrs. Carmichael to the hospital, so maybe they'd be nicer to me. But that kind of gratefulness was short-lived. They might be glad I did the right thing. But it didn't mean they approved of me.

Which was fine by me . . . I didn't want to fit in with the Carmichaels, come to think of it. Changing yourself for others is bull. I didn't need the headache. *And Joely doesn't exactly fit in with your scene either,* I reminded myself as I walked inside to break the good news of my staying to my ma.

"Ricky, phone." Ma handed me the receiver as I banged the screen door behind me.

"It's Coco," a familiar voice drawled, and I quickly pushed thoughts of Joely, of leaving, of quitting school out of my mind. "Wanna shoot some pool?"

"I'd love to," I said, and then I hung up and smiled. I was about to make Ma's day. And then I'd be back to normal life. Playing pool, hanging with my friends. Getting back to where I needed to be.

"He's not here," Carla snapped. "And I don't know when he's getting back."

"Uh . . . could you please just tell him Joely called?"

"Yeah."

I hung up the phone, feeling a total, crushing despondency. It was pointless. I'd left three messages with Carla, and Ricky hadn't called me back. He was leaving tomorrow. But obviously he wasn't going to say good-bye.

I sat down heavily and thumbed through the TV guide, desperate to do something for fear that I would just cave and rush over to Ricky's, wait for him to get home like some kind of stalker. I was dying to see him.

But apparently the sentiment wasn't mutual.

"Let's go, Joely. Mom's waiting." Dad interrupted my thought flow.

"Okay," I mumbled, heaving myself off the couch. I should have felt excited. We were going to the hospital to see Mom and Mary. But instead I just felt like crawling into a hole. I felt sorry for myself. And I wished I knew what to do. Should I just give up on Ricky? Bag the idea of even staying friends? How was I supposed to know? I had so little experience with boys.

And I had no one to bounce my feelings off of. In another lifetime, that person could have been my mom. Other girls had moms who helped them figure these things out. But not me. My mom was totally wrapped up in her other daughter.

And although I couldn't blame Mom or Mary, I couldn't help the way I felt.

Alone.

Mary is five days old. She and Mom are coming home tomorrow, and I should feel excited, but my mind is on something else. To be specific, some*one* else.

Ricky's in Chicago by now. And I'm moping. Megamoping. I know I have to get over it, or else my summer will be ruined. I mean, it's probably for the best that Ricky and I aren't in touch. We're too different.

And even if we weren't, he's gone now, so it's a moot point.

I have to forget about Ricky and focus on the other people in my life. But that's none too easy either. For starters, all my friends are leaving town. Catherine's going to her cabin in Wisconsin. Shelby's headed for the Mathlympics in a few days. I would have been going too. But since Mary came early, I guess I'm stuck here.

God, I'm acting like such a martyr! Mom said I could go to the Mathlympics! *I* was the one who volunteered to stay home! Why?

Because I have responsibilities now, that's why. And I know Mom needs me. Which should make me feel good on some level, but it doesn't. Because my life basically sucks.

I predict the world's worst summer—how could it not be? No sleep because of the baby. No friends. No Ricky.

July 2

Hi, Carmichael,

How about this postcard of the Chicago skyline? Cool city, I think.

But I wouldn't know. Still in Edenvale.

What are you doing July 4? Feel like checking out the fireworks at the lake? Let me know.

Ricky

Eleven

Joely

"H I . . ." I TRIED not to look too ruffled at the sight of Ricky, once again looking incredibly gorgeous. This time he wasn't dressed up at all. Just jeans-and-T-shirt style for our evening at the lake. But he still looked incredibly cute, cute enough to make me feel all jumpy inside and turn my lips dry, despite the gloss I was wearing. "Come on in," I chirped brightly, trying to look chilled out and casual. But I felt anything but relaxed as Ricky came into the house.

Maybe it was the memory of our last attempted date, which almost ended in a home delivery of my sister!

Or maybe it was that totally out-of-nowhere surprise postcard asking me to the fireworks. The postcard that stated Ricky hadn't left after all. And still wanted to see me.

Or maybe it was the fact that I didn't have the

faintest clue what had changed Ricky's mind about me, about moving, about going out on a date. Nor did I even know if he was going to Chicago after all!

To cut a long story short, I knew nothing.

Nothing except the butterflies in my stomach and the sparkle brimming underneath my terrified smile. I was nervy, I was confused, but I was also thrilled. Finally the date was happening. And I had a new A-line red gingham summer dress to prove it.

"Hello, Ricky." Mom greeted Ricky with her warmest smile as I walked him through to the kitchen, where Mom sat holding Mary while Dad made dinner.

"Hello." Ricky smiled, and I could see he was self-conscious even though he tried to hide it. Just as I could see that underneath Mom's smile, she still wasn't wildly overjoyed that I was headed out on a date with Ricky. I knew she was grateful to Ricky. That part was clear. She'd even sent him a note thanking him for getting her to the hospital.

But I also knew that grateful as she was, that didn't change how Mom felt about my dating Ricky. She was still worried about me dating such a "tough guy." Even though she was doing her best to conceal her anxiety in front of him.

"Ricky, this is Mary," Dad said, grinning as Mom held up the baby. "She just came home yesterday."

"Hi, Mary." Ricky took one of Mary's tiny hands in his, and she stared up at him with her huge eyes.

And that's when the conversation kind of died

in midair. I could see Dad struggling for some way of smoothing things over, something to talk about to take the pressure off the moment, but Dad wasn't the big talker of the family.

Luckily Ricky didn't seem to notice—he was still looking at Mary. But I knew it was time to leave. Which was a shame. I'd have liked my parents and Ricky to get along well. Even just for this one night. Too bad. I picked up my handbag and got ready to leave, my mouth hardening into a thin, determined line. My mom might not be into my date with Ricky, but I wasn't going to let her spoil it.

"Can I hold her, Mrs. Carmichael?"

Ricky's request stunned not only my mom, but me too! I'd thought he'd be ready to hotfoot it away from my parents ASAP, but instead he wanted to hold Mary!

"Well . . . I . . ." My nonplussed mom smiled and looked from Dad to Ricky to me. ". . . Sure!" she said brightly. She handed Mary to Ricky, but although she kept her smile, I could see Mom was scared silly. She'd barely even let *me* hold Mary!

"Hi . . . ," Ricky murmured as he lifted Mary into his arms, and for one awful, paralyzing moment I wondered if he knew what he was doing, holding such a tiny baby barely even out of the incubator. What if he dropped her? What if the guy who'd helped my sister make it safely into this world ended up dropping her on her second day home? *And why do you have to think such stupid, terrible things?* I reprimanded myself. But I couldn't help it. Life just seemed so topsy-turvy lately. At least in my world, everything crazy and scary seemed possible. Bad things as well as good.

But then, just when I was thinking the worst, Ricky put one of his hands underneath Mary's head, and she gurgled. "You've got to support her head," Ricky told me as I looked on. "You know that, right, Joely?"

"Not really," I replied, fascinated by the size of Ricky's huge hand against Mary's tiny head. "But I guess I do now."

And then, was I imagining it, or did I feel the vibe in the room suddenly lift?

I wasn't imagining it. Mom's expression was a combination of pleasure and surprise. She was impressed with Ricky; I could tell by the way she cocked her head when she looked at him. "You're obviously very good with babies, Ricky," she said. "Not to mention mothers in labor!"

We all laughed, and right then I knew that this was a pivotal moment. A turning point for me and Ricky and my family. His holding Mary just right had done the trick. He was in with my parents now.

And I felt great.

Ricky

"Everything's good here, but the special tonight is veal. And that's the best," I said to Joely as she pored over her menu.

She looked up and snapped her menu closed. "Sounds delicious."

I liked that about Joely. She was decisive. She could also go with the flow. And she wasn't a vegetarian, I was relieved to see. A lot of rich kids are vegetarians, and personally I think it's stupid. . . . But Joely was cool, and at that moment I felt really okay, sitting with such a pretty, easygoing girl in my parents' restaurant, listening to old jazz on the jukebox . . . about to have a good meal. Things were good.

Mostly.

I knew Joely had a lot of questions. I could see it in her eyes. Obviously she wanted to know why I wasn't in Chicago. And whether or not I was even going. Heck, *I* wanted to know the answer to that too. But I didn't. Yet.

"So . . . are you still going?" Joely echoed my thought stream. "I mean, you were supposed to be gone by now."

I ripped a chunk of focaccia bread and dipped it into the bowl of olive oil between us. "Yeah, I was supposed to be going. But I decided to hold off. Think things through."

Joely nodded, then she also ripped a chunk of bread. "Why didn't you call me?" she blurted. "And then suddenly I hear from you. What's up with that?"

I looked into Joely's clear, inquisitive yes and felt like such a dip. Joely was so to the point, whereas I was all over the place. One minute ready to bust out of town, the next unable to follow through. One moment ignoring Joely, the next asking her out on a date.

"I'm sorry," I said heavily, staring at the bread basket. This was an uncomfortable one. I didn't feel like opening up my insides to show Joely what a confused guy I was, but I didn't see how I could avoid it. "I guess I needed my space. To think about stuff. You wouldn't understand," I finished lamely. "You're always so sure of yourself. Of your life."

I folded my arms and stared into the olive oil, suddenly wondering whether going on this date had been the right move. Being with Joely was already making me feel inadequate. She had her stuff all figured out. High school. College. Joely's future was golden and defined. Mine was . . . how would I know? I didn't know my butt from my elbow!

"You think *I'm* sure of myself?" Joely's question brought me out of myself, and as she brushed her dark hair away from her eyes, I could see the total disbelief in her eyes. "I'm sure of my *life?* Ha!" Joely shook her head vigorously. "That's a funny one."

I shrugged, praying Pop would appear with the antipasti before too long. The conversation was heavy, and it was making me nervous. Still, I needed to clear the air with Joely, so I forced myself to speak my mind, tell her why I'd been so unsure about the date.

"I guess I wasn't sure that going on a real date was such a good idea," I admitted finally. "I'm not blaming your mom or anything, but when that date went wrong, it kind of felt like fate intervening . . . or something."

"I know what you mean," Joely murmured. "I thought the same thing too."

Well, at least we agree on that! I thought, relieved to see that Joely didn't think I was being stupid. "Even the very first time I asked you out, I wasn't sure it was a smart move," I continued, then immediately regretted it. What kind of a thing was that to say to a girl on a date?

But Joely didn't throw the bread at me. In fact, she seemed quite calm when she asked me why I'd been unsure. I think she knew as well as I did, but I guess we were in full disclosure mode, for better or worse.

"I'm not a fool, Joely," I said quietly. "I know your parents have been judging me since the first time they laid eyes on me. And I don't know . . ." I leveled my eyes at hers. "Maybe you have too. And maybe you guys are right. Maybe there are too many differences between us."

"Maybe," Joely murmured. "So why am I here, then?" she finished softly.

I smiled. This part I was sure of. I didn't know much right now, but I knew how to answer that question: "Because I knew I had to find out on my own. If there are too many differences between us, we'll find that out. But judging the situation before it happens is wrong. It's like judging someone's character by their wardrobe. And so if I didn't ask you out, I'd be the worst kind of hypocrite."

Joely grinned then, and for the first time this evening I noticed how the soft candlelight brought out golden lights in her hair. "I'm glad you're taking the risk," she said shyly.

"You gotta take risks," I said, not taking my eyes off Joely. "Sometimes you bite the dust. But sometimes . . ."

Right then our antipasti arrived. Artichoke. And as we started eating, we decided we weren't that different after all. We'd both been unsure of each other, but we were both prepared to take a chance and see what would unfold.

Oh yeah, and we both liked artichokes.

And as Frank Sinatra piped up on the jukebox, I felt like for once, everything was going my way. Frank seemed to be reinforcing that Joely and I had something in common. And the night was off to a real good start.

Joely

"I'm glad you brought a blanket," I said to Ricky as we sat on the grass lawn around Piper Lake. It was a balmy evening, the perfect night to share a blanket with someone and watch Fourth of July fireworks lighting up the sky.

"There's the first firework," Ricky murmured, pointing at a tiny firefly circling near me. "Edenvale's always had a big budget for fireworks," he kidded.

170

"Fireflies have it easy." I was thinking out loud more than actually speaking. "All they have to do is light up their butts when they like another firefly. That sends the signal. There's no confusion."

Yikes! Mortified, I realized I'd just said something highly embarrassing. Why? Because I was a freak. I squeezed my eyes shut, wondering if Ricky thought I was the dork of the century.

But he didn't seem to care. "Just a fired-up butt," Ricky agreed, and then we both laughed as the firefly circled another firefly.

"Nothing to it," I whispered as Ricky's hand suddenly covered mine. Meanwhile my heart felt like it was spinning in my rib cage! The feeling of Ricky's hand on mine was electric. And I'd be a liar to say I wasn't mind-numbingly nervous right about now. I couldn't help it; I was so inexperienced. . . . *What if*—

But before I could finish my terrified thought, Ricky squeezed my hand and shot me a concerned look. "Why so tense? Your hand just went ice-cold."

"I—I . . ." I searched around for something to say. But right then I knew it was stupid to hide my true thoughts. Ricky had been honest with me at the restaurant. The least I could do was be honest back.

"I've been nervous to go out with you. Because you're way more . . . experienced than me, as you know," I blathered, gulping for air and thankful only that the darkening evening could hide my flaming face. I was basically telling Ricky I was a virgin. True, but kind of embarrassing to admit to someone like Ricky.

171

"So why are you here with me if you're so nervous?" Ricky whispered, brushing a strand of hair from my cheekbone.

Good question, my panicked, jumping heart thudded back at me. But I did have an answer. I think Ricky just wanted me to say it: I was ready to take a chance. Walk on the wild side.

Except I wasn't. I didn't want to lose my virginity yet, and I didn't know how to say it without sounding like a supreme dork!

But right then, I didn't have to say it. Because suddenly Ricky's lips touched mine and everything swirled into this one, long, heavenly second where thinking dissolved and all I could feel was the soft but urgent pressure of Ricky's mouth on mine. . . . *Wow* . . . nobody had ever kissed me so tenderly before, and I felt like I was turning into a human fondue in Ricky's arms, my hands fluttering across his broad back as his strong arms wrapped tightly around me, his hand stroking the skin at the base of my neck, making me shiver with pleasure.

When we finally broke apart, I stared at Ricky with total dizzying amazement. The greatest kiss of my life had just taken place! I hadn't even seen it coming. It had totally taken me by surprise. Like everything else in my life lately!

"Joely," Ricky whispered, pulling me down onto the blanket so that I was lying across his chest, his hand stroking my hair. "You don't have to worry. You can trust me. I'll never pressure you into doing anything you're not ready to do." Ricky shifted, propped himself up on one elbow, and we locked eyes. "We'll just go at our own pace," he finished, stroking my cheek with his fingertips.

But even the feeling of Ricky's fingertips grazing my cheek sent me into the most heady, swooning, sparks-in-my-stomach feeling I'd ever experienced. It made me feel woozy and charged at the same time. It made me feel wild and terrified at the same time too. *Our own pace,* I thought worriedly. *What's that going to be? What if Ricky decides to go to Chicago? Does that mean we—*

But just as I began to analyze and break everything down, the first firework shot into the sky in a shower of purple sparks, followed by red Catherine wheels and red, white, and blue sea-anemone-shaped bursts of fire.

And as we sat in silence, holding hands and watching the light show, I forced my mind away from analysis and decided to just be in the moment. And I realized then that sometimes in life it's better just to let things unfold without deciding in advance how things ought to go.

And I realized something else too as I sat at Piper Lake with Ricky. I realized that this was the best date ever. Whoever said "opposites attract" knew exactly what they were talking about. . . .

Twelve

IT'S BEEN ALMOST six months now, and Ricky and I are still going strong. Who'd have thought . . . ??? But then, who'd have thought a lot of things? Like my parents having a baby . . . and turning out to like Ricky! (I'd go so far as to say my mom actually *loves* Ricky because he's so good with Mary!)

And who'd have thought that Carla would turn out to actually (kind of) like me? Or at least, tolerate me.

So much has happened. . . . Ricky decided to stay in school. His grades are still questionable, but he was the star of the school play this year: *A Streetcar Named Desire*.

And there are even more surprises: like the fact that I love being a sister. Everything is so different than I'd thought it would be. For one, I don't have all the responsibility. Mom is coping really well, and although sometimes things get a little hairy and crazy at home, I always remind myself in those moments to be grateful for Mary. Because if it weren't for her, Ricky and I would never even have talked in the first place!

So yeah, things are good. My grades are back up where they used to be, and I have a really great boyfriend. Sure, not everything's perfect. I'm not totally accepted into Ricky's circle of friends, and although he doesn't say it, I know Ricky thinks my friends are kind of nerdy. But I've learned that none of that is really important. What matters most is how we are together.

And together we're great. We've each made slight changes for each other (Ricky's stopped smoking . . . or at least he *says* he has, and I don't lecture him about studying). But neither one of us is trying to be someone we're not.

So what's next? I don't know. . . . It's definitely possible that Ricky will go to Chicago after school. As for me, my parents still want me to go to Princeton. They both went there, so they're really pressuring me. . . . So the big question is, will Ricky and I be forced to separate? I don't even want to think about it.

So I've decided not to. Sometimes you just have to leave things up to fate. Which I'm okay with. After all, fate has worked in my favor before. It brought Ricky to me. And Mary. Yup, as my parents have demonstrated so dramatically, you can't always plan the future. But sometimes the best things in life are surprises!

Do you ever wonder about falling in love? About members of the opposite sex? Do you need a little friendly advice but have no one to turn to? Well, that's where we come in . . . Jenny and Jake. Send us those questions you're dying to ask, and we'll give you the straight scoop on life and love.

DEAR JAKE

Q: *How are you supposed to tell if a guy likes you? Let's say a guy talks to you whenever he sees you but never asks you out. What does that mean?*

LK, Chattanooga, TN

A: Sorry, but this is a toughie. He could be chatting you up because he likes you as a friend, or he could be chatting you up because he likes you romantically but is too shy to ask you out. I suggest you look for little clues that speak to you and decide from there.

Q: *I'm totally crushing on a guy named Paul. He's sooooo cute! We're sort-of friends, meaning that he's in a couple of my* classes and every now and then we talk about something like homework or the teacher. I'm dying to ask him out, but what if he says no?

PT, Fair Lawn, NJ

A: Now you know how guys feel! If you ask him out, there's always the possibility he'll say no. But there's also the possibility he'll say yes. Those are pretty good odds.

Q: *I work in a yogurt shop at the mall. The owner's son is the store manager and I have a huge crush on him. He's always flirting with me, but when people make jokes about us hooking up, he always gets very serious and says that he would never get involved with an employee. I really feel like we have a strong connection. Do you think I should ask him out?*

TR, San Diego, CA

A: It's always wise to follow your heart as long as you're prepared for the consequences. Keep in mind that your crush is the owner's son, and that he's answering to a higher authority. It's quite possible that his father has warned him against on-the-job romances, and rightfully so— they can get pretty sticky. Another option might be to wait until you find another job, and ask him out then.

DEAR JENNY

Q: *I have a crush on my math teacher. All my friends think he's incredibly good-looking (he looks like a movie star). I'm getting bad grades in his class because I can't concentrate on anything but his gorgeous face. Should I tell him how I feel?*

JC, Toledo, OH

A: Once I had a crush on my social studies teacher, and I found myself staring at him more than I found myself listening to him. That's a pretty good indication that a crush is just a crush—I was crushing on him the way I would a movie star or a rock star. I kept my crush to myself, and in a couple of weeks it was gone. The good news is that I started listening and did better in class!

Q: *Why does my older sister hate me? Whenever I see her in the hallways at school, she ignores me. When she brings friends over the house, she acts like I'm not even there. I'm three years younger than she is, and I'm always nice to her.*

KC, Springfield, MO

A: I'm sure she doesn't hate you. In fact, I'll bet she loves you very much. Your question reminds me of how I treated my younger brother when we were in middle school. I acted like I didn't know him! I didn't want my friends—or the guy I liked—to think I was chummy with a "kid," and I wanted to seem "older," so I acted like a jerk. I suggest telling your sister that the way she's acting is hurting your feelings. She may not include you when her friends come over, but she may start smiling at you in the hallways.

Q: *My best friend is tall and skinny with blonde hair. I used to love hanging out with her because we have such a great time together, but lately, it hasn't been so fun for me. No matter where we go together, guys stare at her and give her all the attention. It makes me feel like I'm invisible. I hate feeling that way, and I don't know if I should stop hanging out with her or not. What do you think?*

PG, Boston, MA

A: It must be really hard for you to feel like your friend gets all the attention. But the truth is that you have your own unique qualities that make you special in your own way, and someone is bound to notice them. The world will always be full of people who are smarter, faster, funnier and prettier than you, but life's not a contest. Just concentrate on your own good time and don't let all the attention she's attracting take away from your fun. Also, just because someone notices her first doesn't mean he might not end up preferring you.

Do you have any questions about love?
Although we can't respond individually to your letters,
you just might find your questions answered in our column.

Write to:
Jenny Burgess or Jake Korman
c/o 17th Street Productions,
an Alloy Online, Inc. company.
151 West 26th Street
New York, NY 10001

Don't miss any of the books in *Love Stories*
—the romantic series from Bantam Books!

SUPER EDITIONS

TRILOGIES

LOVE STORIES: HIS. HERS. THEIRS.

Coming soon:

BFYR 232

He was my **parents'** worst nightmare . . . but my dream.

"Hey, Carmichael!" Ricky called out in his gruff, sandpapery voice. He was standing near the fountain with some of his friends. Cool, scary, older-crowd people. I was so embarrassed to be seen in the mall with the parents. On a *Saturday,* no less!

"Hey!" I waved at Ricky and noticed my parents exchange "that look." Every kid knows that look: the big warning signal in that international parent language of coded gestures and expressions. The look that says: Here comes trouble, and our daughter is walking straight toward it.

Maybe because I grew up in a very focused, career-oriented house, I've pretty much been on the straight and narrow all the way. Did I mention I never date the "wrong" guys? Did I mention I never date? (Okay, I've had a few dates, but I'm not exactly the most experienced junior out there.)

So normally, I wouldn't be a point of interest for someone as edgy as Ricky Lenci. But right then I was. And for a moment that seemed like the only thing that mattered. Yeah, my parents were all pale and fidgety, and I could see Ricky's posse looking me up and down, half amused and half critical that he'd even know a "goody-two-shoes" like me. But I didn't care. I could only be excited, especially since Ricky was walking over to me . . . and my parents!